EXPLORER ACADEMY

THE DOUBLE HELIX

TRUDI TRUEIT

UNDER THE *Stars*

NATIONAL GEOGRAPHIC

TO MY MOM AND DAD, FOR LIGHTING THE PATH WITH LOVE, LAUGHTER, AND A LITTLE PIXIE DUST —T.T.

Since 1888, the National Geographic Society has funded more than 12,000 research, exploration, and preservation projects around the world. The Society receives funds from National Geographic Partners, LLC, funded in part by your purchase. A portion of the proceeds from this book supports this vital work. To learn more, visit natgeo.com/info.

NATIONAL GEOGRAPHIC and Yellow Border Design are trademarks of the National Geographic Society, used under license.

For more information, visit nationalgeographic.com, call 1-800-647-5463, or write to the following address:

National Geographic Partners
1145 17th Street N.W.
Washington, D.C. 20036-4688 U.S.A.

Visit us online at nationalgeographic.com/books

For librarians and teachers: ngchildrensbooks.org

More for kids from National Geographic: natgeokids.com

National Geographic Kids magazine inspires children to explore their world with fun yet educational articles on animals, science, nature, and more. Using fresh storytelling and amazing photography, *Nat Geo Kids* shows kids ages 6 to 14 the fascinating truth about the world—and why they should care. **kids.nationalgeographic.com/subscribe**

For information about special discounts for bulk purchases, please contact National Geographic Books Special Sales: specialsales@natgeo.com

For rights or permissions inquiries, please contact National Geographic Books Subsidiary Rights: bookrights@natgeo.com

Designed by Eva Absher-Schantz
Codes and puzzles developed by Dr. Gareth Moore

Hardcover ISBN: 978-1-4263-3458-0
Reinforced library binding ISBN: 978-1-4263-3459-7

Printed in China
19/PPS/1

PRAISE FOR THE EXPLORER ACADEMY SERIES

"A fun, exciting, and action-packed ride that kids will love."

—J.J. Abrams, award-winning film and
television creator, writer, producer, and director

"Inspires the next generation of curious kids to go out into our world and discover something unexpected."

—James Cameron, National Geographic
Explorer-in-Residence and acclaimed filmmaker

"...a fully packed high-tech adventure that offers both cool, educational facts about the planet and a diverse cast of fun characters."

—*Kirkus Reviews*

"Thrill-seeking readers are going to love Cruz and his friends and want to follow them on every step of their high-tech, action-packed adventure."

—Lauren Tarshis, author of the I Survived series

"Absolutely brilliant! Explorer Academy is a fabulous feast for mind and heart—a thrilling, inspiring journey with compelling characters, wondrous places, and the highest possible stakes. Just as there's only one planet Earth, there's only one series like this. Don't wait another instant to enjoy this phenomenal adventure!"

—T.A. Barron, author of the Merlin Saga

"Nonstop action and a mix of full-color photographs and drawings throughout make this appealing to aspiring explorers and reluctant readers alike, and the cliffhanger ending ensures they'll be coming back for more."

—*School Library Journal*

"Explorer Academy is sure to awaken readers' inner adventurer and curiosity about the world around them. But you don't have to take my word for it—check out Cruz, Emmett, Sailor, and Lani's adventures for yourself!"

—LeVar Burton, actor, director, author, and host
of the PBS children's series *Reading Rainbow*

"Sure to appeal to kids who love code cracking and mysteries with cutting-edge technology."

—*Booklist*

"I promise: Once you enter Explorer Academy, you'll never want to leave."

—Valerie Tripp, co-creator and author
of the American Girl series

"...the book's real strength rests in its adventure, as its heroes...tackle puzzles and simulated missions as part of the educational process. Maps, letters, and puzzles bring the exploration to life, and back matter explores the 'Truth Behind the Fiction'...This exciting series...introduces young readers to the joys of science and nature."

—*Publishers Weekly*

"Both my 8-year-old girl and 12-year-old boy LOVED this book. It's fun and adventure and mystery all rolled into one."

—Mom blogger, The Beckham Project

SCIENCE AND EVERYDAY LIFE CANNOT AND SHOULD NOT BE SEPARATED.

—Rosalind Franklin (1920–1958)

30.3285° N   I   35.4444° E

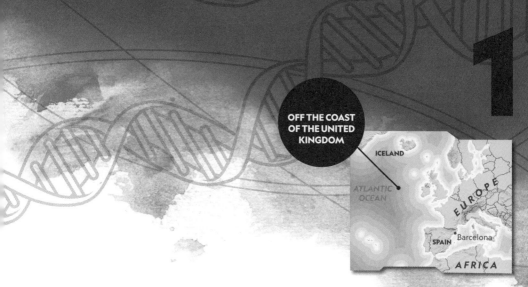

OFF THE COAST
OF THE UNITED
KINGDOM

ICELAND

ATLANTIC
OCEAN

EUROPE

SPAIN Barcelona

AFRICA

RUBBING THE SLEEP from

his eyes, Cruz glanced at the screen of his paper-thin gold wristband. 5:51. *Shoot!*

"Security off. Lights on, low," hissed Cruz so he wouldn't wake his roommate. Flinging off his comforter, he scurried to his dresser, pulling off his pajama top as he went. Blinded, Cruz stubbed his toe on the corner of a chair. He stifled a yelp as he wrestled free of his top. Cruz tugged open his top dresser drawer and grabbed a pair of socks. One drawer below that, he whipped out some jeans and his favorite faded orange *Surf's Up!* tee. He was hopping around the cabin, one leg in his jeans, when Emmett Lu lifted his head from the pillow.

"What's going on?" Emmett glanced at his own wrist. "We're not late for class."

"No, but I'm late for Aunt Marisol." Cruz fell backward on his bed so he could wriggle his other leg into his pants. "The helicopter's coming at six."

"I thought you said goodbye to her last night."

"I did." But wide awake at 2 a.m., Cruz had changed his mind. His dad was missing. Nobody had seen or heard from him in days. Aunt Marisol was flying to Kauai to help in the search for him. That was all that mattered. *That* was where Cruz belonged—not here on board *Orion*, studying and traveling with the rest of the freshman class of

5

Explorer Academy. "But now I want to go with her," said Cruz.

He fully expected Emmett to disagree. Emmett would start listing all the reasons why Cruz should stay: He'd get in trouble for leaving the ship, he'd fall behind in his classes, he'd miss out on their next mission, he'd be letting down Team Cousteau, and on and on...

"Okay," croaked Emmett.

Buttoning his jeans, Cruz froze. That was it? Emmett's emoto-glasses were on his nightstand. Without the shape-shifting frames to reflect Emmett's feelings in color and form, Cruz wasn't sure what his room-mate was thinking. Did he mean "okay" as in, *Go get 'em, I support you a hundred percent*? Or "okay" as in, *Go ahead, but I'm telling you it's a bad idea*? Cruz watched a groggy Emmett slide on his emoto-glasses. In seconds, the frames morphed from flat lime ovals to dark purple circles with pulsing pink streaks. *Yes!* It was the first one.

Emmett yawned. "You packed?"

"Nope." Cruz swung to sit upright and unrolled his socks. "I was going to do it when I got up, but my alarm didn't go off."

"The alarm on your OS band? It didn't go off? Is that even possible?"

Their Organic Synchronization bands, aka Open Sesame bands, measured vital signs, general health, physical activity, brain waves, and growth patterns. The bands' security features gave each student access to every place explorers were allowed to go on the ship. How could a simple alarm not have activated on such a technological masterpiece? Answer: operator error.

"It is when you forget to set it," admitted Cruz.

Throwing his navy-and-white-pinstriped comforter aside, Emmett jumped out of bed. Scurrying to the closet, he flung open the doors, grabbed Cruz's duffel bag from the top shelf, and started filling it with clothes from Cruz's drawers. He yanked Cruz's uniform jacket off its hanger and tossed it to him. "Call her. I'll get your toothbrush."

Pulling on his left sock with one hand, Cruz tapped the comm pin attached to his jacket with the other. "Cruz to Marisol Coronado."

"Marisol here."

He heard an engine in the background. *No!*

"Aunt Marisol, are you still on board *Orion*?"

"I am, but..." The rest of her sentence was drowned out by the *whoosh-whoosh-whoosh* of helicopter blades.

"Wait! Aunt Marisol, wait for me!" There was no time for the right sock. Dropping to his knees, Cruz grabbed a shoe half sticking out from under the bed. The other shoe was next to the box that contained his mother's things. He pushed the box farther under his bed, then stood, cramming his feet into his sneakers.

"Taryn's gonna kill you." Emmett zipped up Cruz's duffel bag.

Explorers were not supposed to leave the ship without permission. Cruz had broken that rule once already during their stop in Iceland. Taryn Secliff had warned him not to do it again, and disobeying his dorm adviser was never a good idea.

"I know." Cruz shoved his arms into his jacket. He grabbed Mell, his honeybee drone, tucking her into an outer pocket.

"I'll handle it. You know Taryn. Hard outer shell, marshmallow center." Emmett slung the strap of the bag over Cruz's shoulder. "*Zù nǐ hǎoyùn,*" he said. It meant "good luck" in Chinese, which Cruz was going to need if he hoped to make it to the top deck of the ship in four minutes. Emmett opened the door, his glasses streaked turquoise and yellow.

"Thanks, Emmett. I'd have had to leave without my stuff if you hadn't—"

"Just go!"

Cruz rushed past his roommate and down the empty passage. He had almost made it to the elevator at the other end when he heard Emmett call his name.

"What?" Cruz shouted, not glancing back.

"I forgot to pack underwear."

Snorting, Cruz nearly hit the wall. He caught the corner and swung around it, launching himself into the two-deck atrium. Cruz charged up the starboard side of the curved grand staircases to the empty

7

third-deck lounge, then up another flight to the fourth deck. He thought he heard someone following him—probably one of the security guards trying to get him to slow down. Nice try. By the time Cruz hit the set of stairs leading to the bridge deck, he was panting, but he had one more deck to go. He took the last flight two steps at a time.

The oval observation roost on the weather deck of *Orion* was cozy yet still had room for a few nubby olive green chairs and a big rug with a fall leaf pattern. Portholes looked out over the helipad—a flat landing zone that was labeled *EA* in letters so big Cruz was sure they could be spotted from space. Hitting the top step, Cruz squinted against bright floodlights that lit up the deck. He could make out a chopper with *Explorer Academy* painted on the side. He heard a noise behind him. "I'm sorry I ran, but—" Cruz spun to face his accuser. "Hubbard?"

"*Woof!*" replied the West Highland white terrier, bouncing in his yellow life vest.

Winded, Cruz put his hands on his hips. "How did you get out of Taryn's cabin?"

Hubbard cocked an ear as if to answer, *Beats me.*

Great! Cruz was going to be in even bigger trouble when his adviser awoke to find her dog missing. "Hubbard, go home." He tried to sound stern.

The little white dog lowered his head.

"Right now." Cruz pointed to the stairs. "Go, Hubbard."

Hubbard let out a whimper. It melted Cruz's heart.

The helicopter's engine was revving. Out the window, Cruz could see a gap between the landing skids and the deck. They were taking off!

"Forget that last order," he said to the Westie. "Stay, Hubbard! Stay!"

Spinning, Cruz punched through the door and raced across the pad. Once Cruz was on board the chopper, he'd call Emmett to come for the dog. "Wait!" he yelled at the rising yellow bird, waving both arms.

A blast of wind slapped him. Hard. Suddenly, Cruz was staring into darkness and struggling to breathe. He was flat on his back, the zipper of his duffel digging into his shoulder blade. It felt as if every last ounce of air had been pushed from his lungs. A minute later, still gasping, he saw a face hovering over him. Aunt Marisol's long, dark hair swirled around her chessboard-print raincoat. "You okay?" she shouted above the whirring engine.

Cruz tried to answer but couldn't get any sound to come out. He'd never been kicked in the chest by a bull before, but he had a feeling this was probably what it felt like. Slowly, he pushed himself up. Taking his duffel, his aunt helped him to his feet and motioned to the door of the roost. Cruz understood. She held up a finger to the pilot to signal she would return. As they made their way inside, they heard the chopper's engine powering down.

"What do you think you're doing?" demanded Aunt Marisol the second the door closed behind them.

"I... You... We..." rasped Cruz.

His aunt glanced down at his bag before tossing it into a chair. "I guess it's pretty obvious, isn't it? You were coming with me."

Hubbard trotted over to them.

Aunt Marisol's jaw dropped. "You were going to bring Hubbard, too?"

"No! I ran up here... turned around... there he was."

"I'm not surprised." Her lips turned up at the corners, but only briefly. "Taryn's going to kill you, you know."

"I know." She now had two good reasons for it.

Aunt Marisol's grin faded. "Cruz, I'm sorry, but you can't come."

"Why not?" He was still hoarse.

She glanced around before hissing, "You know why." Aunt Marisol meant he needed to keep looking for his mother's cipher. Cruz had uncovered two of the eight pieces engraved with the formula for the

9

regenerative serum his mom had created while working for the Synthesis, a secret scientific branch of the Society. So far, Cruz had managed to stay one step ahead of Nebula, the drug company that had killed his mother to stop her from developing the formula and was now bent on destroying all traces of it. "Cruz, you're the only thing standing between Nebula and your mom's work," said his aunt.

Cruz rubbed his right thumb against the rose-colored double-helix birthmark on his left wrist the way he always did when he was wrong and someone else was right. It was true. Petra Coronado had programmed her holo-journal to unlock for one person: Cruz. Only her son could access the clue to find the next piece of the cipher. This was no time to put everything on hold, especially with Nebula out there, waiting to strike. Who knew how much time Cruz had before they did?

"The only thing I care about right now is finding Dad," cried Cruz.

"Of course." Her voice softened. "I know how you feel, Cruz. I'm feeling the same way. But you have important things to do. *Here.* You can't ignore your responsibilities. And you have my word that I'll do everything I can to locate your dad. He is my brother, after all. I'd walk through fire for him."

"I know, but..." How could Cruz make her understand? His mother's death seven years ago had been the worst thing that had ever happened to Cruz. Without his father, he didn't know what he would have done. His dad had been there for him through every surfing competition where moms lined the beach to cheer on their kids, through every nightmare that shook Cruz from sleep, through every birthday and holiday and *any* day when Cruz missed his mom so much he was sure his heart would snap in two. Cruz had been there for his dad, too. They had a strong bond. Even now, one never let more than a few days go by without calling or texting the other. All of Cruz's texts and calls to his dad over the past several days had gone unanswered. Something, he knew, was terribly, terribly wrong.

"Besides, while I'm gone," his aunt was saying, "I was counting on you to assist Dr. Luben—"

"Dr. Luben? From the seed vault?" Cruz liked the English archaeologist, who had given the explorers a tour of the Svalbard Global Seed Vault in Norway.

"Yes, he was gracious enough to step in for me on short notice," explained his aunt. "However, it's been years since he's led students on an expedition."

An expedition!

"Where?" pressed Cruz.

"I...uh...can't say."

"It's a secret?"

"Not exactly. All I can tell you is that you'll learn more when you reach Barcelona."

Spain! They were going to Spain!

"I wish I could tell you more." She bit her lip. "I wish I could *go*. It looks like we'll have to wait a little longer to do a dig together. Anyway, I'm sure Dr. Luben will do an excellent job, but this is your class's first venture into archaeological fieldwork and I'd sleep better knowing one of my top explorers is here to lend a hand. Plus, Archer will be kind and tell me what I want to hear—teachers have a way of doing that—and I want to know how things are *really* going." Her forehead crinkled. "So, will you do this? For me?"

Aunt Marisol rarely asked for a favor. And since it was clear she wasn't going to budge on letting him go with her, he might as well help her out. "All right," surrendered Cruz. "But you have to be honest with me, too. I want to know what's going on at home—even if it's bad."

Swallowing hard, she nodded. "Okay. It's a deal. No secrets. Now I've really got to get out of here or I'm going to miss my flight." She opened her arms.

Cruz gave her a hug.

"It'll be okay," she whispered, planting a kiss on the top of his head. "We'll find him."

He hoped so. Suddenly, tears were clouding his vision. When she released him, Cruz quickly wiped them away.

Aunt Marisol gathered up her hair and tucked it into the back collar of her coat. "When are you going to open the holo-journal for the next clue?"

"Tomorrow, I guess. I want to wait for Lani." Cruz had made a promise to himself that he would never open his mom's journal for a new clue without Lani. They may be 7,000 miles and nine time zones apart, but they were still best friends. "Sailor, Emmett, and I will video call Lani after the Halloween party," said Cruz.

"Tell Lani I'll see her soon." The plan was for Cruz's best friend from back home, Leilani Kealoha, and her mom to pick up Aunt Marisol at Lihue Airport, in Kauai. "I'll call you when I get there."

"Aunt Marisol?"

Her hand on the latch, she glanced back.

"Be careful."

She gave him the smile that always made him feel completely special. Completely loved. "You too."

Scooping up Hubbard, Cruz went to the middle porthole to watch his aunt leave. As she hurried across the helipad, the wind caught her long black-and-white-checkered raincoat, billowing it out behind her like the flag at the end of a car race. Except this wasn't the end.

Nowhere near it. Cruz was scared. For her. For his dad. For himself. The three of them had always been a team. Together, he knew they could face any obstacle and overcome any challenge, but apart...

Well, Cruz had never been without at least one of them at arm's length. Until now.

He wondered if this was how Emmett, Sailor, Bryndis, and the rest of the explorers felt. None of them had family on board.

Aunt Marisol climbed into the chopper and the engine roared to life, the rotor blades becoming a blur. The helicopter gently lifted off.

Cradling Hubbard under his left arm, Cruz waved with his other hand. The deck's lights were bright. He couldn't see Aunt Marisol through the windshield. Wasn't sure she could see him, either. Still he kept waving, even as the chopper turned and headed east toward Ireland. Cruz dropped his hand only when the bird's red tail beacon vanished in the clouds.

The lights on the weather deck were dimming, the black sky turning dark blue. The smell of bacon tickled his nose. It wouldn't be long before the rest of the explorers would be up. Cruz looked down into a pair of chocolate-chip eyes. Feeling a heart jump beneath his hand, he untwisted a tangled zipper tab on a tiny pocket of the dog's yellow life vest. "Guess it's just you and me now, Hub."

A pink tongue curled up to lick his chin.

Cruz slung the strap of his duffel onto one shoulder and, holding Hubbard close, went downstairs to face the day.

2

THAT MORNING, before first period was over, every explorer on board *Orion* knew Aunt Marisol had left the ship. What they didn't know was why. And, like any dogged explorer, each student was determined to find out. During the break between conservation and anthropology, Cruz found himself cornered in the third-deck lounge.

"Is your aunt quitting the Academy?" asked Ali.

"No," said Cruz.

"Is she sick?" pressed Matteo.

"She's fine."

"Is she taking Dr. Hightower's job?" asked Zane.

"Of course not. You guys, come on!"

"So, it isn't true?" Sailor put a hand to her cheek. "She didn't run off with Captain Iskandar to Paris to get married?"

"No!" cried Cruz before he realized she was kidding.

Dugan was studying Cruz, a devilish grin brewing. "This oughta be interesting."

Cruz didn't flinch. He wasn't about to take the bait.

Emmett, unfortunately, was a more trusting fish. "What ought to be interesting?"

"Seeing how Coronado handles not being teacher's pet," drawled Dugan.

"Cut it out." Sailor gave him a scowl. "You know Cruz works as hard as the rest of us."

Dugan opened his mouth but was interrupted by the chime on his tablet. All their tablets were ringing. It was time for second period.

Passing Cruz, Dugan snorted. "Let's see how you do, hotshot, now that you're just one of us lowly students."

"Ignore him," Bryndis whispered to Cruz.

"I'll try," said Cruz, but he wondered, how do you ignore someone who you're supposed to be working alongside? They were teammates, after all.

"Or we could toss him overboard," muttered Sailor.

"Sailor!" Bryndis rolled her eyes.

"Hey, he could use the flotation device we all have in our jacket lining," she pointed out. "And I'd throw a sandwich in after him. I'm not completely heartless."

Matteo slapped Cruz on the back. "Trouble on Team Cousteau?"

"Not a bit." Cruz puffed up. "We're good. Better than good. We're . . . we're supremely fantastic."

"Uh-huh," said Matteo, spinning on his heel to go to class.

Emmett snickered. "Supremely fantastic?"

"Sorry." Cruz scrunched his nose. "It's the first thing I could think of."

"I get it."

They may have been explorers, but the 23 students on board the Academy's flagship vessel were also competitors. Everyone worked, individually *and* as part of their team, to earn high scores on their schoolwork, excel at sports and games, and impress the faculty. Every team wanted to be the best and every explorer was vying for the North Star award, the honor given at the end of their first year to the explorer who showed the most potential. Matteo was on Team Magellan, Team Cousteau's biggest rival for the top spot. However, Team Galileo and Team Earhart could never be counted out. Team Cousteau had to appear to be a strong unit. If Matteo, or anybody else, saw even a tiny fracture, they would use it to their competitive advantage.

Entering anthropology class, Cruz saw Dr. Luben standing in the front of the room next to a table filled with assorted bones, fossils, and artifacts. Dr. Fanchon Quills, their tech lab chief, was beside him. Cruz grinned as he slipped into his seat behind Bryndis and Dugan and between Emmett and Sailor. If Fanchon was here, they must be getting a cool new gadget. Plus, it was fun to see Dr. Luben again. Cruz's first memory of the scientist was watching him zip into the parking lot of the Svalbard Global Seed Vault on his snowmobile, spraying a huge fantail of snow behind him. Dr. Luben had taken the explorers on a tour of the seed vault he'd helped design. He'd explained the importance of safeguarding the world's future food supply in the event of a global catastrophe. Back then, in a black turtleneck, jacket, and ski pants, the scientist had reminded Cruz of an Olympic athlete. Today, however, wearing a crisp white dress shirt, purple tie, and gray dress pants, he looked more like a lawyer.

"Good morning." Dr. Luben's radio voice filled the room from corner to corner.

"Good morning," the explorers answered.

"As you can see, I am *not* Dr. Coronado." His smile softened his square jaw. "I'm Archer Luben, and I'll be filling in while your regular instructor takes some time to deal with a family situation. She'll be back on board as soon as she can. I grew up in Canterbury, in Kent, about fifty-five miles east of London. I studied paleobotany and archaeology at the University of Cambridge. My specialty is space archaeology, and I'm looking forward to sharing this area of study with you. Let's see, what else can I tell you about myself? I like to heli-ski, hike glaciers..."

Sailor was tapping Cruz. "Space archaeology? He looks for artifacts on other planets?"

"No." Cruz chuckled. "He uses space satellites to look for archaeological sites *on Earth.*"

"Ohhh."

"...so, without further ado," Dr. Luben said, sliding a hand through thick wheat blond hair, "let's kick things off with a pop quiz!"

The room went deadly still.

"Joking!" he cried. "Bad sense of humor. You'll learn to live with it. I hope. Relax, there will be no surprises today. We're going to pick up right where Dr. Coronado left off, which means we have a guest speaker. Please welcome your esteemed science tech lab director, Dr. Fanchon Quills."

They applauded.

"Thanks, Dr. Luben. Hello, explorers!" Fanchon hurried around the table, her red flip-flops making a *splick-splack* sound. Over jeans and a pink tee, she wore a sunshine yellow apron with a picture of a grinning white daisy wearing sunglasses. Her caramel curls, the ends dyed bright purple, spilled over the top of a wide giraffe-print headband. Fanchon held up a green device. It looked like a pear sliced in half from top to bottom. "You're all familiar with this, right?"

"Yes," said Cruz, along with the others, flipping open his tablet to take notes. Last week, Aunt Marisol had devoted an entire class to Fanchon's PANDA, or Portable Artifact Notation and Data Analyzer. The device could identify the origin, type, and age of fossils, bones, teeth, pottery, and most every other kind of artifact.

A few rows from Cruz, Felipe Rivera had his hand in the air. Felipe was on Team Galileo. Cruz hadn't gotten a chance to get to know him very well, though he hoped to. Felipe was cheerful and friendly, and he often carried around thick books on cool topics like holo-game design and spy gadgetry. Cruz knew Felipe was from Chile. He also knew, first-hand, that Felipe was a talented classical violinist. Felipe roomed with Kwento Osasona in the cabin next to Emmett and Cruz's. Whenever Felipe practiced his violin, they could hear him through the wall. He was quite good!

Fanchon nodded to Felipe.

"Professor Coronado gave us a whole lesson on PANDAs," Felipe said politely. "We know how to use them."

"That may be, but you don't know how to use *these*," said Fanchon, grinning. "My assistant, Dr. Vanderwick, and I have recently made some improvements to the device, which I think you'll find helpful. You may have learned in biology that DNA, or deoxyribonucleic acid, contains the genetic instructions all living organisms need to develop, function, and reproduce."

There were a few snorts and snickers. Cruz saw Zane elbow Matteo, who elbowed Ali.

"DNA can be found in every cell of every living organism, even plants," continued Fanchon, giving the boys a warning look. "It's also found in the cells we shed, such as hair, sweat, saliva, and skin. In fact, you slough off about thirty thousand skin cells every hour! DNA can survive for hundreds of thousands—even millions—of years, depending on environmental conditions. Now, thanks to our upgrade, your PANDA unit can scan artifacts, fossils, bones, and teeth for plant and animal DNA. If it finds a trace, the software will attempt to analyze and identify it."

"Whoa!" Cruz bounced in his seat.

Emmett's glasses were two green circles sprinkled with yellow dots.

"The analysis may not always be successful," continued Fanchon. "The DNA may be too old or contaminated, but when it works, it's pretty amazing. Let me show you. Watch closely. Once I'm done with the demo, we'll hand out the PANDAs and let you try it for yourselves." Fanchon picked up one of the fossils, a cross-section of a lumpy gray rock. "Say you've discovered this coprolite. First, you'd do just as you always have. You'd press the blue button labeled 'ID,' wait for the 'scan now' signal to appear on-screen, and scan the piece. Within a few minutes, the PANDA would provide complete background info on your item. You'd know what it is, where it came from, and how old it is. Now, to check for DNA, you'd press this yellow button, marked 'DNA,' wait for the 'scan now' indicator, and do a second scan of the object. If no trace of cellular information is found or it's too contaminated to be processed, it will simply indicate that on the screen. If, however, DNA has been discovered, you'll be alerted by a soft tone—"

"Ehhhhh." It was Dugan. He had let out a yawn with one of those I'm-totally-and-completely-bored sounds.

A giraffe-print headband turned. Pink lips formed a tight line. *Splick-splack. Splick-splack.* Flip-flops headed in the direction of Team Cousteau.

"Uh-oh," mumbled Emmett, his glasses turning to maroon rectangles of worry.

The sandals came to a halt in front of Dugan, who'd at least had the sense to shrink down in his seat. Sitting behind his teammate, Cruz could see the fire in Fanchon's eyes. She crooked her finger. "Mr. Marsh, perhaps you'd care to help demonstrate."

"Yes, ma'am," said Dugan sheepishly, getting to his feet. He followed Fanchon to the front of the room. Turning, he gave the class an apologetic look.

Several kids shook their heads. Cruz was among them, though he felt sorry for Dugan. His teammate was quite smart. Dugan was usually among the top scorers when it came to their projects and homework assignments. It was the people part that gave him trouble. Dugan was always quick to say exactly what was on his mind. Sometimes too quick. If you had an idea and Dugan didn't like it, he'd tell you—and not always nicely. He could be rude and rigid and self-centered and nitpicky and competitive and jealous and . . .

Exhausting. That was it, plain and simple. Dugan could be very exhausting. If only Dugan would take a minute to think before he spoke—or, in this case, yawned—he'd get along better. Not that Cruz could tell him any of this. Dugan also didn't take constructive criticism well. But then, neither did Cruz. Now that he thought about it, he didn't really know anybody who did. Criticism was criticism, no matter how kindly it was put.

Fanchon handed Dugan a PANDA unit and the fossil, then turned to the explorers. "While Dugan identifies the fossil, let me finish my explanation. After you scan for DNA, the readout will give you a comprehensive analysis of the results. If DNA has been found on the piece, you'll have about fifteen seconds to decide if you want to proceed to the next phase..."

Cruz heard a low hum. He looked around to try to figure out where it was coming from, but as quickly as it came, it disappeared.

Fanchon was still talking. "...if you don't want to go on, hit the 'stop' button and you're done. If you do want to continue, do nothing, and— Wait, Dugan, did you do the ID scan first?"

"No. I figured we already knew what it was, so I—"

Raaawwwwwr!

A mighty roar nearly sent Cruz out of his chair. Out of the corner of his eye, he saw a big cat bounding across the front of the room! However, this was no ordinary house cat. A mountain lion, maybe? Reaching the port wall, the sandy-colored animal turned, revealing two front teeth the size of bananas. A saber-toothed cat! Weren't they... extinct?

Rearing back, the animal lunged toward Dugan, who hit the floor stomach first. The cat landed next to the table of artifacts, then turned toward the students. The explorers screamed as they watched it leap for Bryndis, its massive paws stretching out...

Eeeeek!

...and passing right through her!

"A hologram!" called Cruz as the animal cleared his right shoulder. "It's a saber-toothed cat hologram."

"The correct genus name is *Smilodon*," interjected Dr. Luben. He was peeking out from behind a pole. "*Smilodon* means 'knife tooth.' Did you know saber-toothed cats aren't tigers at all? These extinct cats are distantly related to modern lions and cheetahs."

"You okay, Dugan?" Fanchon knelt beside the explorer, who was flattened to the floor like a piece of gum after a concert. She shut off his PANDA unit, and the *Smilodon*, which was still bolting around the room, vanished.

"What happened?" gasped Dugan. He rolled over.

"You didn't follow my instructions."

"Sorry, Fanchon."

"That's all right." Fanchon helped him up. "Next time, though, please do *exactly* as you're told. Go ahead, take your seat."

Lowering his head, Dugan shuffled back to his desk.

Cruz glanced at Sailor. She was resting her chin in her hand, looking both annoyed and mildly amused. "Overboard," she mouthed.

Cruz bit his lip to keep from smiling.

Fanchon cleared her throat, and everyone settled down. "As I was saying, if DNA has been discovered in or on your artifact and you choose to proceed to the final step, a *digital representation of the organism* will be projected for your review. The PANDA analyzes all of the data it collects, including forensics, and, when possible, the software will give you an approximate description of the activity the lifeform was engaged in shortly prior to its death. The activity could be two minutes, two hours, or two days before death. Sorry, we haven't honed the technology to be that specific yet. Remember, we're dealing in thousands, even millions, of years. Anyway, the fifteen-second delay gives you time to halt the display of the holographic image in the event it's not a convenient time to view it or you decide you'd rather not see, say, a *Smilodon* engaged in battle. This is why it's wise to identify your object *first*, so there are no ... uh ... surprises."

The whole class laughed. Well, most of the class laughed. Sailor, Cruz, and Emmett gave one another worried looks. This was not the impression they wanted Team Cousteau to make on Fanchon or their new professor.

"By the way, if the unit detects human DNA, I have programmed the protocol to hypothesize and project accompanying hairstyles, clothing, and accessories, as necessary," added Fanchon. "We have promised your parents, after all, to give you a wholesome education."

More giggles. And snorts.

"Another volunteer?" prompted Fanchon.

Everyone politely raised their hands, and she selected Zane Patrick from Team Magellan.

"This time, let's use this Mesozoic-era ginkgo leaf fossil," Fanchon said to Zane, picking up a chunk of limestone from the table. "We should be safe with a plant, unless a dinosaur was chewing on it before it fossilized."

As he watched Zane scan the cream-colored rock, Cruz's hand went to the two interlocking pieces of stone he wore around his neck hidden beneath his shirt. His mother had engraved her formula into black marble. Would any of her DNA, he wondered, be on it? Probably not. But maybe. It would be fun to see if the PANDA could pick up any traces. Of course, he couldn't scan it here. Not in front of everyone. The PANDA units were issued to the explorers only for training or fieldwork, so they weren't allowed to take them back to their cabins.

Maybe another time...

The email icon on Cruz's tablet was blinking. It was probably Aunt Marisol checking in to let him know she was on her way to Kauai. It was a long journey—7,000 miles—and would take her two days. She had a stop in New Jersey and an overnight layover in LA. It was against the rules to check mail during class. He would only take a quick peek, just to make sure her plane had taken off okay. Tapping the mail icon, he began to read...

Sailor was nudging him. "Think Dugan even knows what a coprolite is? Dibs on getting to be the one to tell him he was holding fossilized cat poop. Cruz? Is something wrong?"

Speechless, Cruz tipped his tablet so Sailor could see the message for herself.

> *We have your father. He is unharmed and will remain so, provided you tell no one about this note and follow our instructions. You will be given more details at the explorer Halloween party. Don't miss it. No tricks.*

Sailor gasped. "Nebula?"

"Who else?"

As they looked on, the note on Cruz's screen blurred, then turned into thousands of tiny squares. One by one, each of the pixels faded to black. It was as if the message had never been there at all.

Poof!

3

STARING at the door, goose bumps rippled down Cruz's arms.

Nebula, he knew, was on the other side of that door. Waiting for him.

This was supposed to have been a fun night in the CAVE celebrating Halloween. Some of the explorers had never heard of the holiday, which fell on October 31, so Taryn had given them a brief history. She'd explained how the festivities first arose from Ireland's Gaelic harvest feast of Samhain, when the Celts believed the ghosts of the dead returned to Earth. It was customary to calm the spirits by offering them treats. When the Irish immigrated to America, they brought the tradition with them. Over time, the ghostly holiday had evolved into a night where younger children went door-to-door collecting candy (trick-or-treating), while older kids and adults went to costume parties with spooky themes, games, and food. Ever since Taryn had told them that *Orion* would host a Halloween party, Cruz had been looking forward to it. Now he wanted it to be over.

Cruz glanced at his two friends, all dressed up in their costumes. Emmett had parted his hair in the middle and slicked down both sides with gel. A fake black mustache kept falling off his upper lip. Wearing a gray tweed suit and high-collared white shirt, Emmett was dressed up for the party as inventor Nikola Tesla. In case nobody figured it out, he was also carrying a miniature Tesla model car. Sailor was going as scientist Marie Curie. She wore a long black cotton dress that swept the floor behind her boots. She'd piled her thick hair up into a bun. In case nobody got *her* costume, she had pinned to her collar a plastic yellow triangle with a three-pronged black fan—the warning symbol for radioactive material. Cruz wore a purple-and-white Hawaiian-print shirt, a pair of blue board shorts, and sandals. He did not, however, have on the one thing he usually wore: the cipher. It felt strange, not having the lanyard around his neck. But he had no intention of handing the stones over to Nebula until he knew, for sure, his dad was free. It wasn't easy to leave the cipher behind, even though it was in a safe place. He hoped. Under his arm, Cruz carried a surfboard that was a third the size of a real one. He'd made it with the 3D printer he and Emmett shared. He'd painted the board to look like the North Atlantic right whale calf he'd talked to during Operation Cetacean Extrication. The art had taken him a whole week to finish. Now all the hours he had put into the surfboard no longer mattered. He was here for one reason: to get his father back safely.

"Ready?" asked Emmett, and when Cruz nodded, he lifted his wrist to the security camera. The device read his Open Sesame band, and a moment later, the door began to move.

The mini CAVE, as they called the simulator on board *Orion,* was smaller than the regular CAVE back at Academy headquarters but identical in every other way. Combining holographic imagery, thermal radiation technology, 3D printing, and climate controls, the CAVE created a lifelike experience. It could be programmed to reproduce any environment in the world, from a bustling street in Paris to a remote jungle in the Amazon. Some aspects of the CAVE were real, such as atmospheric conditions and necessary solid objects (these were created using a 3D printer). Other features were virtual but felt real, like holo-thermal videos. Reach for an image and the heat from your body reacted with it to produce a sensation, tricking your brain into thinking you were touching an actual object. Cruz could have studied all the science behind it, the way Emmett did, but preferred not to. It was a bit like watching a magician. It was more fun if you didn't know how the trick was done.

Cruz felt his friends' eyes on him. Emmett and Sailor were waiting for him to go into the CAVE first. He could see only darkness ahead. Drawing in a sharp breath, Cruz stepped inside the compartment. His teammates followed, the door sliding closed behind them. Almost immediately, the trio was engulfed in a thick fog. Between the mist and the darkness, Cruz couldn't see the hand he'd raised in front of his face. It smelled like dirt. And popcorn balls. A wolf howled. Sailor's fingers were digging into his right arm. "Easy, Sailor." Cruz winced. "It's only a simulation."

"I know that," she said calmly from behind his left shoulder.

The grip loosened. The clouds parted, and a full harvest moon revealed Emmett's face. "Sorry." He shrugged.

As the mist cleared, Cruz realized they were standing on the rickety porch of an old house. The structure was leaning to the right, yellow paint peeling off the siding in curly tendrils. The porch light flickered. A ghostly young girl with red eyes and seaweed hair leaned out the attic window. "Help me, Cruz! Please, Sailor! Help me, Emmett!" she moaned, before slipping back behind torn curtains.

"Taryn did a good job with this program," said Emmett, swatting at a bat that was trying to land in his hair. "This place is pretty creepy."

The front door swung open with a spine-chilling creak. "Welcome, guys and ghouls!" cried Fanchon. She was wearing an apple green apron that read *Brainy Girls Rock* over a purple tie-dyed tee and ripped jeans. A tiger-print scarf was wrapped around her head. Plastic safety goggles, chunky earrings, and a pair of orange flip-flops completed the look. In the dim light, it took Cruz a moment to see he'd been wrong. It wasn't Fanchon at all.

"Taryn!" Cruz laughed. "Great costume."

"Thanks!"

"You didn't borrow anything from Fanchon's real lab, did you? 'Cause I can tell you from experience, her sensotivia gel is not very friendly."

"Hey! Are you picking on my lab experiments?" A head with cropped brown hair popped around the door. Wearing a short wig, a red turtleneck with a gold badge that read *Taryn,* and a red-and-gray plaid skirt, Cruz recognized their tech lab chief. She held a half-knitted scarf and a stuffed white dog in a yellow life vest under her arm—Hubbard, of course. Fanchon and Taryn had dressed up as each other!

Once inside, Cruz's eyes roved around the black hexagonal foyer lit in spooky hues of purple and green. Above them, holographic witches flew around a cobweb-covered chandelier on their brooms and cackled with wicked delight.

"Every room has something different to do," explained Taryn. "There's Bobbing for Eyeballs, Wrap the Mummy, Build Your Own Monster, Tombstone Dash, and Mystery Box. Oh, and if a zombie grabs you, you have to go and help haunt the cemetery for ten minutes to spook the contestants running in the dash. Food is in the dining room, but stay out of the kitchen because Chef Kristos is in there and you know how he hates to have anyone around while he cooks." She touched Cruz's arm. "And, you, stop looking so worried. Nobody's grading you. The surveillance cameras are off. None of your professors are here. This is for explorers only. So relax and have *fun.*"

"I will," he said, trying to squelch the panic in his gut.

They heard creaking boards.

"More guests!" Taryn rushed to answer the door again.

Cruz, Emmett, and Sailor cautiously shuffled toward the center of the hexagonal foyer.

"How are you supposed to find Nebula?" Emmett swiped a cobweb out of their path.

"I have a feeling they'll find me," whispered Cruz, his legs melting a bit with each step.

Cruz had told his roommate about the note he'd received and his suspicion that Nebula had his father. Both Emmett and Sailor had promised to stay close tonight.

They had four choices: turn right into the dining room, go left into the living room, continue straight down a narrow hall, or go up the stairs. They could hear cheering from the living room. Cruz peered in. Ali and Matteo were trying to wrap a mummy. They were competing against Weatherly and Felipe, from Team Galileo, and losing badly. About a dozen explorers had gathered around the competitors to cheer them on.

"Hey, guys!" called Bryndis from across the foyer. She was in the dining room, next to a bubbling cauldron. White foam tubes were coiled around her long-sleeved white tee and matching ballet tutu and tights. She'd made a headpiece out of a couple of the foam tubes. A coating of silver glitter covered everything, even her white blond hair. Bryndis looked like a white-chocolate-covered pretzel, but that couldn't be her costume, could it? Seeing Cruz's puzzled expression, she grinned. "I'm bleached coral. Lame, huh?"

"No! Cool!" Leave it to Bryndis to come up with a clever environmental costume.

She dipped a ladle into the cauldron. "Want some punch, surfer dude?"

"Okay." Having the other explorers around was making Cruz feel a little more at ease. Everybody *was* having a good time. Nebula wouldn't try anything in front of everyone, would they?

"We're out of cups," said Bryndis. "There are more in the kitchen—"

"I'll get them," said Sailor, reaching for the door handle.

"Sailor, that's not—"

But it was too late. The moment Sailor cracked the door, two greenish hands popped out of the pantry and latched on to her arm. A holographic zombie began to wrap chains around her wrist. "Bloody undead," groaned Sailor as the zombie led her away. "See you in a bit. I hope."

"Bring cups on your way back," giggled Bryndis. She turned to Emmett and Cruz. "So what do you guys want to do? Build a monster? Bob for eyeballs?"

"Taryn said something about a mystery box," said Emmett. "Is that a game?"

"Uh-huh. You wear a blindfold and put your hands in a box to

identify what's inside. I've done it already. It's fun! Come on, I'll show you where it is." She reached for Cruz's hand.

He felt a jolt of static electricity. Bryndis jumped, and he knew she'd felt it, too.

Bryndis led them out of the dining room and down the narrow hall. "Taryn says the explorer that guesses the most items correctly gets a prize at the end of the party. I got five right. If you miss even one, you're out."

"How many are there?" asked Emmett.

"Nobody knows. They're holo-thermal, so as long as you keep guessing correctly, you'll get a new one. Last I heard, Felipe had gotten the most: ten. Here it is." Stopping in front of a silver door, Bryndis nodded to the square light next to it that was off. "The light's not on, so nobody's inside. Only one person can go in at a time. Who wants to be first?"

Cruz was about to volunteer, when he felt a tapping on his chest. Seconds later, his honeybee drone flew out of his shirt pocket. Hovering near his head, Mell flashed her golden eyes.

"Security breach," said Emmett, glancing at his OS band. "Somebody's tripped a sensor in our cabin. I don't have my tablet—didn't think I'd need it tonight. It's probably a false alarm, but I'd better go up and check it out." He looked at Cruz, his eyes widening behind square gray frames. "You'll be okay?"

"Yeah. Sure." Cruz tried to sound confident, but an uneasy feeling crept over him. Their plan to stick together had fallen apart. First Sailor had left, and now Emmett...

His roommate backed away. Slowly. Reluctantly.

Cruz watched him go, then turned to face the silver door. Alone.

"I'll hold your surfboard," offered Bryndis.

"Thanks." He handed it to her.

She smiled. "You've got this."

Cruz took a deep breath and headed inside. The square room was dark but for a narrow spotlight shining straight down on a tarnished old silver box. The box was about the size of a half dozen stacked paperbacks. It was perched on a red velvet cloth that covered a square table. A black satin scarf sat neatly folded beside the box. There was no other furniture in the room. No light fixtures. No windows. No closet. Cruz approached the waist-high table. In the air above the box, silver words in cursive script appeared like winter fog:

*Here's **a** blindfold you must wear.*
*Then reach inside m**e**, if you dare.*
*Close the **lid**, **s**peak what I store.*
*If you're correct, **we**'ll play **o**nce more.*
*Many have **t**ried my mixed-up riddle.*
***Un**scramble your thoughts to **de**code my middle.*

Cruz put the scarf over his eyes, tying it tight at the back of his head. He didn't want to be accused of cheating. He placed both hands on the sides of the lid and tipped it back. Carefully, he dipped his fingertips into the box until he felt something soft. Cold. Squishy. He slid his hand along the slimy surface, just to be sure, then closed the top. "Spaghetti noodles," he said clearly.

He waited. Would anyone tell him if he was right or wrong? Nothing was happening.

Hmm. The instructions had said if he was right he would get to continue, so either the box would open again for him or it wouldn't, right? It was worth a try. Cruz reached for the lid. It opened. He put his hand inside. This one he knew right away. He let the hard triangles sift through his fingers.

"Candy corn."

As he continued, the items got harder and harder to figure out. Popcorn. Sliced olives. Flower petals.

Number six was tricky. Cold and mushy, it fell apart in his hands. Snow? Was he allowed to smell it? The rules hadn't said he couldn't. Cruz brought it up to his nose. *Ah!*

Cruz closed the box. "Watermelon," he proclaimed.

He was lifting the lid for a seventh time when he felt something clamp on to his shoulder. A claw? No, a hand. Cruz's pulse quickened.

"Do not move," said a digitized voice from over his shoulder.

"O-okay."

"Do not speak until you are told," demanded the altered voice. Cruz couldn't tell if it was male or female.

Cruz let his right hand drop from the box. He slowly slipped it inside the pocket of his shorts, his palm closed around a baseball-size orb. The octopod was a defensive weapon Fanchon had created for him based on his mother's research into animal venoms. Press one of the blue rings and the ball released a spray that temporarily paralyzed an attacker.

"Talk!" ordered the digital voice. "You have ten seconds."

"Huh?"

"Cruz?" said a familiar voice.

"Dad!"

"I'm here, son." His dad was on the phone. Cruz could feel it being held up to his ear. "Are you okay?" shouted Cruz. He didn't know why he was yelling.

"I'm fine. Other than hurting my wrist. I turned my hand like I did on your birthday last year. What about you?" asked his dad. "Are you all right?"

"Yes. I'm on *Orion*. Don't worry. We'll get you home."

"Cruz, whatever you do, don't—"

The line went dead.

"Dad? *Dad?*"

"That was too fast. It couldn't have been ten seconds," protested Cruz.

"Your father will be released as soon as we have what we want," said the digital voice.

Cruz spun the octopod in his pocket until he felt the beak-like nozzle with his index finger. Spinning it, he found two indentations, one for his index finger and the other for his thumb. Pressing the one under his thumb would release the repellent through the beak.

Someone was grabbing the collar of his shirt. He felt the smoothness of a gloved hand probing the back of his neck. "Where is it?" demanded the voice.

"What?" said Cruz, sliding the octopod upward.

"The cipher. Where is the cipher?"

Stunned, Cruz froze.

"I won't ask again," snapped the voice. "Where is the formula?"

"You . . . you didn't think I'd bring it with me, did you?" he sputtered.

There was a pause, confirming that's exactly what he/she/it thought. Everything was becoming clear. Somehow, Nebula had discovered Cruz's secret—that he wore the two pieces of the cipher around his neck. They had expected him to come here tonight with it. They'd planned to destroy it and then kill both him *and* his father. That had been their mission all along: to get rid of his mother and anyone connected with her. They must have congratulated themselves on such a simple plan. However, Cruz wasn't about to make anything easy for Nebula.

Another hand was on his neck, this one sliding around to his throat. As the glove tightened, Cruz's pulse began to race. He thrust his left elbow straight back as hard as he could, hoping to hit a rib or stomach or anything that would get the attacker's grip to loosen. It worked.

He heard a yelp. Fingers slid from his throat. Pulling the blindfold down over his mouth with his left hand, Cruz spun and raised his right arm. There was no time to aim. He squeezed his thumb and index finger, sending a peacock blue mist over a black mask covered in red jewels. A caped figure doubled over and began to cough. Cruz kept the black blindfold clamped to his mouth so he didn't accidentally inhale the spray. He sped for the door, flung it open, and ran smack into Sailor. "Nebula..." he gasped, his hand still over his mouth.

She hit her comm pin. "Sailor York to security. We need help in the haunted house in the CAVE. Now!" She turned to Cruz. "Are you okay?"

Still gasping, he put a hand to his neck. "I think so..."

Dugan was coming toward them. He was dressed in a foam taco costume. "Is that the mystery box room?"

"Yes, but you can't go in," snapped Sailor.

"How come?" Dugan went for the doorknob. "The light's not on. Taryn said I could go in if the light was off."

"No!" Cruz reached out for Dugan. "Somebody dangerous... in there—"

"Hey, hands off the lettuce, man. It took me forever to glue this stuff on." Jerking free of Cruz's grip, he pushed open the door.

"Security!" They heard the call from the front foyer.

"Here!" shouted Sailor. "Officer Dover! We're down here!"

Dugan had taken the opportunity to slip inside. He poked his head back out. "Whatever joke you're trying to play, it's not funny."

"What do you mean?" asked Cruz, his heart still thrashing in his chest.

Dugan opened the door. "There's nobody in here."

Sailor and Cruz peered in.

Dugan was right. The room was empty.

4

▶ **"WHAT DO YOU** mean we didn't get it? How could this happen?"

"Zebra said there was a bit of a mix-up, but we're handling it," said Thorne Prescott.

He felt ridiculous, talking to an oil painting of flowers. As usual, his boss preferred to keep his identity hidden, which was why today, Hezekiah Brume had pointed his phone at a canvas of canary yellow poppies in a dark brown vase. Three red poppies had been tucked into the side of the vase, almost as an after-thought.

"It's a minor setback, sir," said Prescott.

"What about your end?" Brume was asking about their captive.

"Smooth as silk," Prescott answered confidently.

It was true. Marco Coronado was safe in the master bedroom's walk-in closet. He'd had a hot shower, a change of clothes, and a breakfast of scrambled eggs, toast with jam, and coffee. Prescott had even given him a chance to stretch his legs on the balcony. However, they had to be careful. They would need to keep moving. They couldn't take the chance they'd be spotted by a nosy neighbor, or someone from the botanical gardens next door. Scorpion hadn't realized when he'd rented the place it was so close to a popular tourist destination, but by then it was too late. Things were already in motion. Prescott was annoyed, though not worried. As long as they behaved like normal vacationers and didn't stay too long, everything would go according to plan.

"Komodo and I will be leaving today," said Prescott. "We're taking the sugar—I mean, the shuttle to the airport." He winced

35

at his slip. He had nearly blurted out their next destination: the abandoned sugar mill at the south end of the island. That's what happens when you have too many codes to remember. You make mistakes. Brume insisted that everyone in his inner circle use code names. In their line of work, real names were forbidden to speak and, often, dangerous to know. Brume's code name was Lion. Prescott's was Cobra, for his snakeskin boots. Komodo and Scorpion were assigned to Prescott. Spies Zebra and Jaguar were both on board Orion.

Brume's phone tipped forward. Prescott's boss was standing up. The shot gave Prescott a closer view of the trio of red poppies in the painting. The largest bloom faced upward, its blood-red petals open to the sun. The middle stem hung limp. The last poppy was a small bud. It couldn't have taken more than a brush-stroke or two to create. And yet, it seemed . . . necessary.

"Cobra?"

"Yes, sir."

"The clock is ticking."

Prescott bristled. He knew precisely how much time he had—four weeks. It was plenty of time to get the cipher pieces and get rid of Cruz, though he still didn't know why the kid had to be dealt with before he turned 13. "We'll make it, Lion."

"You'd better," growled Brume. "Or else."

Prescott's gaze dropped to the tiniest red flower on the canvas. Or else what?

5

➤ **"I KNEW IT,** I knew it, I knew it." Sailor was pacing Emmett and Cruz's cabin. "I should not have left you at the party."

"It's okay," said Cruz for the millionth time. He propped up his tablet against the dresser so Lani could see them and they could see her. "I had my octopod—"

"But if you hadn't . . ." said Lani from her bedroom in Kauai.

He put his nose to the screen. "But I *did*."

"But if you hadn't."

Cruz glanced at his tablet. He'd been checking his email every two minutes since he'd gotten back to his cabin, hoping for a new message from Nebula. So far—nothing.

Sailor passed behind Cruz, still pacing. "I should never have left you."

"Me either," said Emmett, turning from his computer. His emoto-glasses were ash gray ovals. "We fell right into their trap."

Cruz tipped his head. "Trap?"

"Nebula must have figured Sailor and I would be stuck to you like glue, so they knew they'd have to get us out of the way. And boy, did they. First they got Sailor with the zombie, then me with our security breach, which, by the way, was a false alarm."

"That might not have been Nebula," said Sailor. "You've had false alarms before, you know, like when housekeeping comes in to vacuum."

37

"Yes, but *somebody* had to trip it." Emmett gestured to his screen. "I've looked at all the video footage from tonight. Nobody was in here. They didn't even jiggle the door, yet *all* the sensors went off."

Cruz was puzzled. "How could that happen?"

"Someone had to have hacked into the system."

Not just someone. Nebula.

"Nebula knew I'd have to investigate since they'd instructed you to be at the CAVE for the party," concluded Emmett. "And that, of course, left you alone."

Sailor stopped pacing. "Yeah, but how did Nebula know Cruz would go into the mystery box room?"

Emmett lifted a shoulder. "We're explorers, aren't we? Not many of us are going to turn down a game like that. And if Cruz hadn't gone in, they probably had a plan for that, too, like slipping him a note or something."

Cruz put a hand to where the cipher pieces usually laid on his chest. "Okay, but how did they know I wear the cipher? Besides Aunt Marisol, you guys are the only ones who know that."

"I think that's pretty obvious," said Lani.

It was? All eyes swung to the screen on Cruz's tablet.

"They saw you," explained Lani. Staring at three confused explorers, she let out an exasperated sigh. "If Nebula hacked into your account to trigger your sensors, couldn't they have hacked into your surveillance system, too?"

"Well . . . y-yes," sputtered Emmett, "but they'd have to get past my firewalls first, and those are impenetrable."

"But if they managed to do it somehow," continued Lani, "then they could have been watching you using *your own cameras*!"

At that, every hair on the back of Cruz's neck stood at attention. He moved slowly toward the bookshelf above his desk, to one of the five cameras Emmett had placed around the room. Each camera was disguised as a conch seashell. Stepping up on his chair, Cruz peered directly into the dark eye of a tiny lens. If Lani was right, Nebula could have been spying on them for days. Or weeks. They could be watching them right now!

"Shut it down, Emmett," ordered Cruz, leaping from the chair. "Shut down the whole system. Now!"

"Check," cried Emmett.

"I'll get a box." Sailor rushed to the closet.

While Emmett tapped at his keyboard and Sailor riffled through the closet, Cruz raced around the room and grabbed the rest of the shell cameras.

"Got one!" Sailor stepped back from the closet with an empty shoebox.

Cruz dumped the cameras into the box, and Sailor slammed on the lid.

"Done!" Emmett swiveled in his chair. "I shut down my account. The system is off—cameras, laser beams, motion sensors, the works."

For a moment, nobody said a word. They all stared at the shoebox in Sailor's hands as if it might explode.

Getting up, Emmett took the box from Sailor. He carried it out to the veranda, shoved it under one of the chairs, then came back inside. "I'll give everything back to Fanchon in the morning. Sorry, Cruz. I thought my protocol was totally secure, but I should know by now that when it comes to Nebula, *nothing* is totally secure."

"Um … it's getting late," said Sailor, glancing at her OS band. "Do you still want to open your mom's journal for the third clue?"

"Yes," answered Cruz. He did, more than ever.

He reached into the lower pocket of his uniform jacket hanging on the back of his desk chair and brought out the flat, square holo-journal. Laying it on the dresser next to Lani's head, he slid the white paper out of the protective sleeve Lani had created for it. Cruz stepped back and waited for the journal to transform into a three-dimensional pointed sphere, which would then emit an orange beam to scan and identify him.

Five seconds passed. Then ten.

Cruz put his hand on the journal. It was his touch that had activated it the first time. Maybe he hadn't held it long enough.

Everyone stared at the flat white piece of paper. Another minute went by. Still nothing.

They could hear Felipe next door, practicing his violin. He was doing scales.

Lani was craning her neck. "Shouldn't something have happened by now?"

Cruz looked at Sailor in the reflection of the mirror. "You don't think...?"

She frowned. "It looked fine in the ice cave, but...?"

"What's the matter?" pressed Lani. "Why isn't it doing its morphing thing?"

Cruz hated to even think it, let alone say it. "It might be... broken."

"Broken?" She gasped. "How?"

Cruz looked at Emmett, who looked at Sailor. None of them wanted to break the bad news.

Sighing, Sailor walked toward Lani. "Before Tripp set off the blast in the ice cave, he threw the journal on the ground and... stomped on it. After the blast and cave-in, Cruz found it in the rubble. It didn't look damaged, but I guess... I guess it was."

"Impossible," proclaimed Lani. "My sleeve is made from reinforced goethite nanofibers, which would have sufficiently protected the journal from Tripp's crushfest as well as the explosion."

There was an awkward silence. Nobody wanted to suggest that, like Emmett's security measures, Lani's sleeve wasn't as perfect as she thought.

"It could have been the cold weather," offered Sailor.

"Or... or..." Cruz was grasping for a reason. "... one of the corners was sticking out of the envelope."

"Or it could be malfunctioning all on its own," said Emmett. "There could be lots of reasons why it's not working."

Cruz turned to his roommate. "Do you think you could fix it?"

"I don't know." His forehead wrinkled. "I ... I could try."

Cruz held out the journal. "Try."

"I can help, too," said Lani. "I mean, if you want me to, Emmett."

"I'll take all the help I can get," he said. "I'll call you tomorrow and we'll get to work."

"Sounds good."

The lights flickered, signaling they had only a few minutes until lights-out. "I'd better go." Sailor touched Cruz's arm. "We'll figure it out. Night, Team Cousteau and Lani."

Lani and Emmett said goodbye.

Once Sailor left, Emmett went into the bathroom to brush his teeth.

"Okay, for real, Cruz"—Lani's face loomed closer to the camera—"how *are* you?"

The fear he'd been squashing down into the pit of his stomach was beginning to rise. Cruz started to pace, following the footprints Sailor had left in the carpet. "I think I may have ruined everything, Lani ... I think my dad may be ..." He shook his head as the terrible thoughts overwhelmed him.

"No, you didn't, and no, he isn't," Lani said firmly.

"Then why haven't they contacted me?"

"They will. They let you talk to your dad, right?"

"Yes, but that was before—"

"And what did he say?"

"Not ... much. We only got a few seconds." Cruz scrambled to think. "He asked about me. I said I was fine and he said, 'Whatever you do, don't' ... and that was it. They cut us off." Cruz looked up at his best friend, helpless. "Don't what? *Don't worry? Don't give them the cipher? Don't screw up and spray paralytic octopus venom into the bad guy's face after they deliberately tell you no tricks?*" Cruz ran his hands through his hair, clawing at his scalp, then, suddenly, stopped. He slowly lowered his arms to stare at his wrists. What was it his dad had said? At the time, something about it had seemed strange, but everything had happened so quickly he hadn't had time to think...

"Cruz?" Lani brought him back to the moment. "What's the matter?"

"On the phone my dad said... It was just weird..."

"What was?"

"I asked him if he was all right, and he said he was, except he'd turned his hand like he did last year *on my birthday*. The thing is, he *didn't* twist his wrist on my birthday. I remember because for my twelfth birthday we went up to the botanical gardens."

"Limahuli or Princeville?"

"Limahuli."

"That's my favorite," sighed Lani. "I love the terraced taro gardens there."

"Me too. After we walked through the gardens, we had lunch at Ke'e Beach, then went on a short hike on the Kalalau Trail." Cruz's mind was whirling. "Dad didn't get hurt at all. I don't get it. Why would he say he did?"

"I don't know. Maybe he sprained his wrist and didn't notice until the next day or something. I did that with my ankle once, playing soccer. I thought I was fine, but when I got home, it started to swell and throb—"

"Lani!"

"What?"

"Turned hand. Limahuli means 'turned hand' in Hawaiian."

She drew in a sharp breath. "Are you saying you think your dad was trying to give you a clue to his location?"

"Could be," said Cruz. "Limahuli is only about twenty minutes from Hanalei."

"There aren't many roads up there. It's mostly forest and the perfect place to hide someone you've just kidnapped." He could hear her tapping on her laptop. "Tiko and I could drive up and check it out after he closes the shop. Oh, by the way, Tiko is running the Goofy Foot while your dad is ... away. He wanted me to tell you that everything is under control."

"Tell him thanks. I know Dad appreciates it, too. Lani?"

"Yeah?"

"Watch your step at Limahuli," warned Cruz. "I don't need you getting kidnapped, too."

She snorted. "You'd better go or you'll be brushing your teeth by the light of Mell. Text me when you hear from Nebula . . . or if you can't sleep."

"Okay."

"Try not to worry." She cringed. "Sorry. I hate it when people say that to me, because trying *not* to do something only means you're sure to do it. Somehow, it'll all work out. I know it will."

"Thanks," he said, but Cruz wasn't nearly as optimistic as his best friend. The same people who had killed his mother now held his father. Would it all work out? Somehow, he doubted it. "Aloha, Lani."

"Aloha."

Cruz checked his inbox again, even though the icon clearly showed there were no new messages. He moved his tablet from the dresser to his nightstand and got into his pajamas. When he came out of the bathroom, all the cabin lights were off, except for Emmett's industrial desk lamp. He'd made it out of an assortment of antique pipes, clamps, and an old Bunsen burner. The shade was a lab beaker with a clear tubular bulb hanging inside. Cruz had nicknamed it the mad scientist lamp.

Cruz turned up the volume on his tablet so he would hear the chime of a message, and climbed into bed. The boys said their good nights and Emmett clicked off the light.

Turning his head on the pillow, Cruz looked at the silver dome on his nightstand. He longed to play the video it contained—the one of his mother and him at the beach when he was a toddler. He resisted the impulse to reach out for it. He didn't want to keep Emmett up. Besides, he knew every second of the video by heart. He could just as easily play it in his head.

"Cruz?" Emmett's voice drifted through the dark cabin.

"Yeah?"

"Your cipher . . ."

Cruz sighed. He had been waiting for this. "You want to know where it is."

"I... I was surprised you took it off, that's all. You always wear it."

"Well, I could hardly bring it with me tonight."

"But you are ... I mean, you are going to give it to them, aren't you?"

"Yes." Cruz was not about to play games with Nebula, not with his father's life at stake.

For a while, Cruz focused on listening to the hum of the engines, hoping they might lull him to sleep. It didn't work. If only he could hear Felipe play Bach's Sonata No. 1 in G minor. The haunting melody almost always put him to sleep. Unfortunately, Felipe usually played it in the early evening, while Cruz was trying to do his homework.

"Cruz?"

"It's somewhere safe, Emmett. It isn't that I don't trust you," he hurried on, "but the more you know, the more danger you're in. Believe me, it's better this way."

Emmett didn't say anything, but in the darkness, Cruz saw him turn away.

Cruz let out a long, tired breath. The last thing he wanted to do was hurt his friend, but with Nebula closing in, he couldn't take any chances—not with the cipher and certainly not with those he cared about. Anyone who knew where the stones were was at risk. That's why Cruz could not tell Emmett his secret: He had entrusted the cipher to the only soul on board *Orion* who wouldn't—or, more accurately, couldn't—tell anybody that he had it.

3, 1 24, 8 14, 10 22, 2

6

"**HUBBARD!**" Emmett knelt in the passage
to greet the little dog in a yellow life jacket. The Westie was carrying his
green rubber ball in his mouth. Cruz and Emmett often stopped on their
way to breakfast to play a few rounds of fetch with Hubbard. The dog
lowered his head to get pets from Emmett, then trotted over to Cruz and
dropped the toy.

Cruz knelt, one hand reaching for the ball coated with drool, while the
other found the little zippered pocket on the side of the dog's life vest. He
unzipped the pocket and slipped his fingers inside. He didn't exhale until
he felt the cool touch of marble. Cruz hesitated. Nebula, he knew, could
be around the next corner. They would always have him in their sights. But
Hubbard? Maybe it was best to leave the cipher right where it was. For now.
Cruz slid the zipper closed. Scratching the Westie's favorite spot behind
his ear, Cruz leaned in to whisper, "Keep it safe, huh?" Cruz tossed the ball
down the corridor, and Hubbard took off after it. The boys threw the ball
a few more times before heading off to eat. The pair waved to Taryn, who
was in her doorway, keeping an eye on Hubbard as she dried her hair with
a palm-size solar dryer. She smiled and nodded as they passed.

On their way up the grand staircase in the atrium, Cruz checked his
tablet. The mail icon was solid. Why hadn't Nebula gotten in touch with
him? This was agony. "I don't get it," he moaned. "What are they waiting
for?"

"They're icing you on purpose," said his roommate. "They want you on edge. It gives them the advantage. Don't give them that kind of power."

Sometimes Emmett sounded more like a spy than an explorer.

Nodding, Cruz tucked the tablet under his arm and vowed not to check his mail for 10 whole minutes. He wished it were Monday, though. At least then he'd have classes to keep him occupied.

"I'll get to work on the journal right after breakfast," said Emmett. His glasses were black trapezoids, meaning he was feeling the pressure. "It could be something simple, such as a glitch in the biometric activator, or it could be more complicated, like the metastasis regulator. If that's out of alignment, I'm not sure I can repair it. That technology is pretty advanced—"

"It couldn't be *that* advanced," cut in Cruz. "Mom created it at least seven years ago."

"Let's just say your mom was ahead of her time. Speaking of time, how much do Lani and I have?"

Yesterday, Cruz had checked the navigational charts, so he knew *Orion* was currently in the North Atlantic, off the southwestern coast of Ireland. He had hoped to have the next clue figured out by the time the ship went through the Strait of Gibraltar in about three days. But now that the journal was out of commission, that was on hold. Cruz knew Emmett was under enough stress as it was. "As much as you need," he answered smoothly.

"So none, then?"

Cruz couldn't help laughing. Emmett was getting to know him too well.

In the dining room, they were met by Chef Kristos. The wiry cook was wearing his usual crisp white double-breasted chef's coat. It never seemed to have a single stain on it. This was truly amazing considering Chef Kristos was always in motion—whisking, chopping, blending, frosting—often, all at the same time! Today, he was behind the buffet server, next to a hot plate, with about a dozen bowls lined up in front of him.

Chef was cracking eggs into a steel bowl with one hand and slowly shuffling a pan over the burner with the other.

"Sweet as!" cried Emmett. "It's omelet day."

Chef Kristos lifted an egg. "What would you like in your omelet, Emmett?"

Emmett surveyed the row of bowls. "Let's see… can I have cheddar cheese, tomatoes, bacon, sausage, olives, onions, and pineapple? Oh, and ham?"

"I do have to leave room in the omelet for the eggs, you know," said Chef Kristos, laughing. "And you, Cruz?"

"Nothing for me, thanks." Cruz's stomach felt like one of Taryn's balls of yarn after Hubbard had gotten ahold of it.

They watched Chef whip up Emmett's omelet, cook it, then slide the fluffy yellow semicircle onto a white plate.

"Thanks, Chef," said Emmett, taking the plate and putting it on the blue tray that Cruz held out.

As they continued down the buffet line, Emmett plucked a container of raspberry yogurt and some sliced cantaloupe from the ice-filled servers and added them to the tray. At the beverage bar, Emmett put a glass of orange juice on the tray. Cruz was about to turn away, when Emmett placed another full glass beside the first. "You should at least have some juice," he said. Cruz didn't argue.

It wasn't yet eight o'clock, so Cruz wasn't surprised to see the dining room nearly empty. Most of the explorers took the opportunity to sleep in on Sundays. Cruz saw Dugan with Ali, Tao, Yulia, Ekaterina, and Matteo seated at a corner table. Zane was the only member of Team Magellan missing. The group was intently listening to Dugan, though Cruz couldn't hear what he was saying. As Cruz and Emmett approached, they all started to get up.

"Morning," said Cruz.

"Morning," answered Team Magellan.

"Hey," said Dugan quietly, though he didn't look at them.

Cruz set their tray down at a clean table. Slipping his tablet out from under his elbow, he laid it down on the table face up and took a seat. Emmett was still standing, still watching the other explorers leave. Cruz didn't have to check Emmett's emoto-glasses to know something was bothering his friend.

"For being a Cousteau, Dugan's spending an awful lot of time with the Magellans," said Emmett, finally pulling out a chair.

"Well, he *is* Ali's roommate."

"What if he's telling them secrets about our team?"

Smirking, Cruz took a sip of his orange juice. "Like how you always lose your socks in the laundry or that Sailor's favorite ice cream is something called hokeypokey? Oh, I know—Bryndis and I talk about farting fish when we're diving!" Cruz laughed, but Emmett didn't.

"I don't like it, that's all," said Emmett, stabbing at a chunk of cantaloupe.

"You know Dugan," sighed Cruz. "He's just..."

They looked at each other. "Different!" they said in unison, nodding and grinning.

Dugan was Dugan, and there was no telling what he would say or do next.

While Emmett ate, Cruz checked his email again. Still no new messa— Wait! The mail icon was blinking. Holding his breath, Cruz tapped it.

Hi Cruz,

Spending the night in LA, then on to Kauai tomorrow. No news about your dad yet, but I have been talking with Hanalei police and am hopeful. They are pursuing a few leads. How are you? How did the first class with Dr. Luben go? Hugs for you and pets for Hubbard.

Love,

Aunt Marisol

"My aunt says they have a few clues about where my dad is," said Cruz.

Emmett glanced up. "What kind of clues?"

"She doesn't say."

"You're not going to tell her about Nebula—"

"No, but I hate keeping things from her. We promised there would be no secrets. If there was any other way . . ."

Emmett gave him a solemn nod.

Cruz emailed his aunt back that he was fine and class went well, for the most part. He told her about Dugan's mistake with the upgraded PANDA unit but that Fanchon and Dr. Luben had handled everything smoothly. He said nothing about the broken journal or kidnapping. He had, after all, only promised to be honest about anthropology class, so, technically, he wasn't breaking his vow. Then why did it feel like he was?

"*Mōrena.*" Sailor plunked her tray down next to Cruz. She had an omelet, cereal, milk, toast, and apple juice.

"*Mōrena.*" Cruz returned the good-morning greeting in Sailor's native Maori. His mouth full, Emmett raised his fork.

Sailor put the plate of toast in front of Cruz.

"What's this?" Cruz looked down at the two slices of golden toast, cut on the diagonal. The four triangles were neatly placed on each side of a small, square crystal bowl filled with strawberry jam. "I didn't order it."

"You didn't?" Sailor took a seat. "That's weird. One of the waiters asked me to bring it over to you."

"Chef Kristos probably told him to." Emmett was working to get a piece of sausage, a sliver of ham, and a couple of olives onto his fork. "You know how he always says we shouldn't skip breakfast."

Now that Cruz thought about it, he *was* a little hungry. He dipped the small knife into the shallow bowl and spread jam over one of the toast points. Cruz took a bite. The sweetness of warm strawberries mingling with the crunchy wheat bread was delicious.

Sailor poured milk over her cereal. "I've been thinking a lot about your problem, and I think I've got a solution."

Emmett's head went up. "You mean, about fixing the journal?"

"No." She leaned in to quietly add, "About the cipher."

"I'm giving them the stones." Cruz took another bite of toast.

"Sure, but"—she gave him a sideways grin—"what if you didn't have to?"

Cruz stopped chewing. "What do you mean?"

"Here's what I'm thinking." Sailor moved in even closer. "Thanks to your surveillance cameras, Nebula probably knows what the cipher looks like, right? So what if we made duplicate pieces that looked exactly like the real ones? Well, not *exactly.* We could change some of the formula but everything else would be like the real thing—same color, shape, size, weight, everything. Then we'd give the fake pieces to Nebula to get your dad back."

Cruz stared at her. "A decoy cipher?"

Sailor's eyes widened. "Why not?"

"But how—"

"We'd give Fanchon one of your stones to analyze, then locate a black marble stone or create one in the lab that's similar. Fanchon could laser-engrave some symbols onto the stones, slice 'em up, and there you go." She flung herself backward in her chair. "You get your dad back *and* you get to keep the cipher *and* Nebula has a completely useless cipher. Problem solved."

"I . . . I don't know." Cruz nibbled on the crust of his toast. "If Nebula suspected for even a second that the cipher was fake—"

"We could do it," broke in Emmett. "It's a brilliant idea."

Sailor grinned. "It is? You never think I have good ideas."

"I never said that."

"You never didn't say it."

"Huh?"

While his friends bickered, Cruz finished his first diagonal of toast and spread strawberry jam on the second. It was an interesting plan, except for one thing . . .

"Fanchon!" burst Cruz.

Emmett and Sailor stopped squabbling.

"We can't trust her," he continued. "Not after what happened with Mr. Rook and Tripp Scarlatos." Both the Academy's librarian and *Orion*'s submersible pilot had turned out to be working for Nebula. Both had betrayed Cruz.

"You're right." Sighing, Sailor reached for her apple juice. "Guess it wasn't such a brilliant idea after all."

"No, it was—is," said Cruz. "What I meant was, if we're going to do it, we'll have to do it ourselves. And I think we can." He plunged the knife into the jam, scooped out a hunk of strawberry, and slapped it onto the bread. "We'll use a PANDA unit to analyze the stone, then create one using our 3D printer."

Sailor beamed. "Sweet as!"

They slapped palms.

Cruz swung to his roommate. "Emmett, what do you think?"

"I think . . ." His voice trailing off, Emmett pointed in front of Cruz. Through the haze of strawberry jam, Cruz realized there was a hand-written note sitting under the square bottom of the crystal bowl. The print was small. Neat. Delicate. With his knife, Cruz pushed the rest of the red jam aside.

THE SPICE BAZAAR
ISTANBUL, TURKEY
SATURDAY, NOVEMBER 14
9 A.M. BRING THE CIPHER.
TELL NO ONE. COME ALONE.
LAST CHANCE

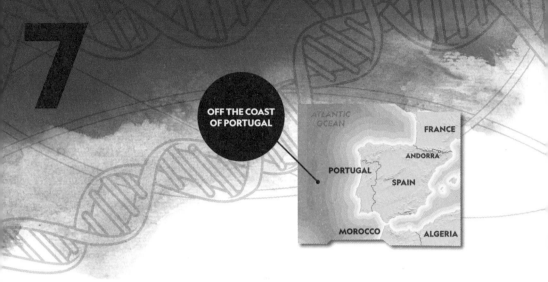

7

PROFESSOR LUBEN had a

mischievous glint in his eye.

It was Monday morning, and Cruz and Emmett had arrived for anthropology only to find their instructor standing outside of the classroom with the door closed. His hands clasped behind his back, Dr. Luben was bouncing on his toes like a little kid eager to open his birthday presents. A couple of the ship's security officers were hovering nearby, too. That was odd. The security guards on this deck usually stayed at their post in the lounge.

"Something's up," Cruz said to Emmett.

"Mmm-hmm," said Emmett, his mind clearly somewhere else. Cruz noticed his roommate's glasses seemed to be stuck on the same color: brown. Cruz knew what was behind the glum attitude. Emmett and Lani were struggling to fix the journal. They had been at it for two straight days (and most of those nights) without success. If the journal couldn't be repaired, everything Cruz's mother had worked for, and had given her life for, would be gone. It was a loss too great for Cruz to consider. Not that he was ready to. Not yet.

Bryndis and Sailor strolled up. "Are we locked out?" asked Bryndis.

"Nope," said Professor Luben, the corners of his mouth turning up.

One by one, the explorers joined the crowd outside Manatee classroom. Dugan was whispering to the explorers he was standing with:

Matteo, Zane, and Yulia—again, all members of Team Magellan. While they waited for the rest of the class to arrive, Cruz checked his tablet for a message from his aunt. She had called him early yesterday to let him know she'd arrived safely in Kauai and promised to update him after she talked with investigators. There was nothing in his inbox this morning from Aunt Marisol, but there *was* something from Lani:

I have to talk to you. It's urgent. WHEN??!!

Good question. It wasn't easy syncing schedules with your best friend when you were always in motion. Cruz pulled up the world time zones chart on his tablet so he could calculate the time difference between Kauai and *Orion*'s current location. The ship was somewhere off the coast of Portugal. The zone on the map showed he was 10 hours ahead. It was 11 p.m. in Kauai right now. If they spoke at 7 a.m. Hawaii-Aleutian standard time, he could catch Lani before she went to school. It would be 5 p.m. his time. Perfect. Cruz typed the message and sent it.

Seeing Felipe jog down the passage toward them, Professor Luben put a hand on the doorknob. "Ah, the last explorer to reach the summit!"

Felipe's face turned red. "Sorry. Am ... am I late?"

"Right on time," answered Dr. Luben, holding up a hand to quiet them down. "Explorers, please enter in single file. Instead of taking your seats, I'd like for you to form a circle around the display at the front of the room, but touch nothing." He opened the door and motioned for them to go in ahead of him. "Move quickly and quietly, please."

Cruz was behind Bryndis, who was behind Sailor. In the doorway, Bryndis turned and gave him a grin as if to say, *Here we go!* Emmett was behind Cruz.

The place was nearly dark. In the front of the room, three ceiling bulbs bathed a long, rectangular wooden box in a warm glow. The painted box had been placed on a glass stand about four feet tall. Security Officer Dover stood behind it near the wall, a contented grin on her face. Approaching, Cruz stumbled over his own feet when he realized what it was: an ancient coffin!

The lid was carved and painted to resemble a beautiful Egyptian woman—most certainly the mummy inside. Aunt Marisol had sent Cruz enough postcards from Africa for him to recognize the signs of early Egyptian art: the eyes and eyebrows done in thick black lines, the large headdress with its bold black and gold stripes, and the draped rows of elegant necklaces decorating the chest. It seemed almost every inch of the box was covered in artwork. Squares of intricate black-and-red hieroglyphs covered the midriff, legs, and feet. Even the spaces had stripes, dots, or a repeating pattern of some kind. As his eyes traveled down the length of the coffin, Cruz's heart dropped. *Oh no!* It was cracked! The break ran across the middle of the lid clear through to the box below. The fracture had been repaired, but a scar remained.

Bryndis let out a tiny gasp. She had seen it, too.

"It must have happened when the archaeologists were excavating the tomb," Cruz whispered to her.

"Too bad," she said.

Once everyone had gathered around the coffin, Professor Luben stepped into their circle. "You are looking at one of three sarcophagi of an Egyptian woman who lived more than two thousand six hundred years ago. It's here because the experts working on its restoration needed some assistance from a couple of Academy scientists. I'll explain more about that in a moment. For now, step up and have a look."

They hesitated.

"Go on," prodded Professor Luben. "You're not likely to get a chance like this again." As the explorers inched inward, their professor held out his hand toward a series of black symbols painted on the coffin, among them a rectangle, a vase, a bird, and a pair of reeds. Cruz knew the reeds represented the letter *y,* but the rest he wasn't so sure about.

"This writing tells us the name of the deceased," said their professor. "Her name was Shesepamuntayesher." He said her name again, slowly, breaking up the syllables so they could learn the pronunciation: "Shez-ep-AH-mun-TIE-ess-HAIR. She had three burial boxes that sat one inside the other, like Russian nesting dolls—this is the innermost coffin, the one that held the body. I can tell by your faces you are long-ing for a peek inside. I'm sorry to disappoint you—there's no mummy. Still, there is plenty to see. You haven't done your Egyptian unit yet, so I'll give you a few highlights. Here, the coffin tells us she is *nebet per,* or the lady of the house. This was the most common title for women in ancient Egypt. There's the falcon-headed god, Thoth, and over here, Hathor, the goddess of motherhood, joy, and love."

"Look, Hathor has an ankh," blurted Cruz. "Sorry, Professor Luben."

"No penalties for enthusiasm in my class, Cruz, especially when you're correct. Do you know what an ankh symbolized?"

"Life," said Cruz.

"Very good."

Professor Luben continued his way around the sarcophagus, point-ing out the various paintings of gods and goddesses, funeral writings wishing Shesepamuntayesher a beautiful burial, and magic spells from the Book of the Dead. When their teacher finished, he turned to them. "Does anyone have any questions?"

Cruz's hand shot up.

"Yes?"

Cruz nodded to the split in the sarcophagus. "I was wondering how that happened. Did someone drop it?"

"No." A shadow crossed the professor's face. "Someone cut it."

The explorers gasped.

"Cut it?" cried Cruz. "You mean ... on purpose?"

"That is exactly what I mean," said their teacher. "Thieves dug up her grave, stole the sarcophagi, and smuggled them out of Egypt. They sawed the boxes into pieces, hid them inside furniture, and shipped everything by express mail to an antiquities dealer in New York. The dealer had the coffins restored, but as you can see, the damage was done. Had the authorities not caught up with him, the dealer would have sold the boxes to a wealthy collector, who may or may not have known how they were brought into the country. This sarcophagus was one of more than seven thousand cultural objects seized by U.S. authorities as part of an investigation into a smuggling network. The smugglers illegally brought in artifacts from a number of countries, including Italy, China, Yemen, and Syria."

"Did you say seven *thousand*?" Sailor gasped.

"I did. And that's the tip of the iceberg."

"Why do they do it?" asked Bryndis. "Don't they know they're destroying history?"

"Why do people steal anything? And yes, they know what they are doing," he said crisply. Shoving his hands deep in his pockets, Professor Luben began a slow journey around the sarcophagus. "Looting is as old as the pharaohs. The thieves often work under cover of night, ransacking tombs and ancient sites for whatever treasures they can find. They'll dig the pits quickly, using shovels, backhoes, and even dynamite! They leave destruction in their wake. For every piece they keep, they destroy hundreds more. The mummies are worthless to them, and so they scatter the bones."

"Dr. Luben?" Felipe slowly raised his hand. "Do you mean ... Are you saying ... Shesepamuntayesher ...?"

"Is lost, I'm afraid," answered their teacher. "If her tomb had been carefully excavated by archaeologists, we would have also likely been able to uncover the objects she was buried with—sheets of papyrus with magic spells, amulets and other jewelry, and painted chests. Also, because it was tradition to bury families together, she would have been laid to rest in a niche near her ancestors with her descendants nearby. All would have had their own treasures with them, too. Properly done, it could have been a priceless discovery. But now all we have is this ..." Professor Luben lifted his head, and Cruz thought he saw the sparkle of tears in his eyes. "It is still an important find, of course, but think what might have been."

No one said a word. They stared solemnly at the damaged sarcophagus.

"Well, we do have one other thing," said Professor Luben. "The sarcophagus was sent here with the hope that Fanchon Quills and Sidril Vanderwick might be able to extract DNA from the wood. It was a long shot, because the body would have been wrapped in linen for burial."

"And did they?" cried Matteo. "Did they find DNA?"

"I don't know." Dr. Luben brought a hand from his pocket. He was holding a PANDA unit. "Fanchon gave this to me just before class this morning. She said it contained the answer." Smirking, he glanced around. "Should we find out together?"

"Yes!" cried the class so loudly, Cruz was sure Captain Iskandar could hear them two decks up on the bridge.

Placing the PANDA on the display stand next to the coffin, Dr. Luben tapped a button. He took a step back. Cruz held his breath.

There! The flicker of an arm. A cream-colored dress. A dark head. Twenty-three explorers stared upward, eyes widening and jaws dropping. It took a few seconds for the complete 3D holo-image of the Egyptian woman to appear.

"Shesepamuntayesher!" whispered Emmett.

Funny thing was, except for the way she was dressed, she didn't look that different from a modern college-age girl. She had smooth, olive skin, deep brown eyes rimmed with black eyeliner, and shoulder-length black hair that was braided in hundreds of small sections. The front braids were swept back and held behind her head with a gold clip. Under a sheer white tunic, she had on a sleeveless cream tube dress that fell to her ankles. She wore no shoes. Walking on the air above her own coffin, she strolled to the end of the display stand and stopped in front of Cruz. Glancing down, she grinned as if she recognized him. Could she see him? No, of course not. And yet...

Cruz couldn't help it. He smiled back.

Reaching out a hand to Cruz, Shesepamuntayesher began to kneel. And was gone.

Cruz remembered Fanchon's explanation that the PANDA units could reveal one of the last activities the life-form was doing not long before death. He wondered how soon after this moment Shesepamuntayesher had died. She didn't seem like she knew her life was about to end. But maybe that's how it is.

For a long while, nobody moved.

"So," said Professor Luben softly. "It's my turn to ask you a question. What are you prepared to do?"

"You ... you mean about looting?" Sailor gulped.

Professor Luben nodded.

Cruz wasn't sure. Was there anything he *could* do?

"No offense," said Zane, "but it's not like we can go to Egypt and catch the bad guys."

"I wouldn't be so sure about that," said Dr. Luben. "True, as a society, it is difficult to catch looters and smugglers and control the global market for the stolen objects they sell. But as explorers, there is a great deal we can do." Stepping through the ring of students, their teacher turned on the holo-projector. A split screen with two satellite maps appeared above them. Cruz noticed that although the images were of the same desert location, they were not identical. The image on the left contained fairly smooth ground with a few pits, but the other showed so many craters pocking the landscape it looked like the moon. "These infrared and laser-generated images were taken of an area south of Cairo, close to where researchers believe Shesepa-muntayesher's tomb was raided," explained their professor. "The image on the left was taken about a decade ago. They image on the right was taken last month."

"What are all those spots?" Dugan asked what they were all thinking.

"Not spots. Holes. They are all the pits that looters have dug."

Cruz was stunned. There were hundreds and hundreds and hundreds of holes!

"We use detailed satellite images to see where people are digging. Based on the photos, archaeologists can estimate the age of a looted tomb and alert the authorities to keep an eye out for antiquities from that time period that come on the market for sale. But, as you can see, it's a huge undertaking."

"We're going to look for looting sites, aren't we?" cried Cruz. "We're going to be space archaeologists!"

"You bet! Lights on, full." As the lights came up, Professor Luben had them take their seats. "Here's what we're going to do. Each team will be assigned a country bordering the Mediterranean that has been victimized by looting. On your tablets, you'll find a link to a tutorial. It will teach you how to scan the satellite imagery and what to look for. You'll then connect with the Society's space archaeology page online, and your team will be given an area within your country to search for looting holes. You'll use the large computerized map tables in the library—they are much easier to see. Dr. Holland has created a schedule for each group, which you'll find on your tablets. As a team, you'll prepare a report of your findings to give orally to the class and a written report for me, which I'll pass along to Society scientists and, perhaps, the authorities."

Cruz looked at Emmett. His roommate's glasses had morphed into lime green ovals with bright yellow streaks of curiosity. *Finally!* That brown color was starting to depress Cruz.

"I've randomly drawn a country for each team to survey," said Dr. Luben, picking up his tablet. "In no particular order, here they are.

Team Galileo, you'll be assigned to Libya. Team Magellan, you've got Egypt. Team Earhart, you'll be scanning Greece, and Team Cousteau, you have Turkey."

Cruz tensed. Turkey was where Nebula had ordered him to go for the ransom drop.

Emmett saw him stiffen. "Luck of the draw," he hissed. "Weird luck, but still luck."

Cruz supposed so.

Dr. Luben was dismissing the class. "Remember, do the online looting tutorial and check your schedules to see when your group is down for map time in the library. Also, you have two reading assignments: one on the archaeology of Spain and another on parietal art. Please familiarize yourself with cave paintings, relief sculpture, and petroglyphs—not saying there's a quiz coming, but there's a quiz coming."

Cruz made a quick note in his tablet about his assignments. In each of their classes, the explorers were reading about Spain so that when they arrived in Barcelona they would be familiar with the country's culture, animals, geography, government, and conservation challenges.

Everyone gathered their stuff and filed out the way they usually did between second and third periods—quickly. The explorers only had 15 minutes to scurry back to their cabins, change for fitness and survival class, and make it down to the CAVE. If you weren't on time, Monsieur Legrand would make you do extra push-ups or sit-ups or something-ups. Cruz knew he should have rushed out with the rest of the explorers, but he wanted one last look at the coffin.

"I'll catch up," Cruz said to Emmett, before making his way to the front of the class.

The intricate artwork, the hieroglyphics, even the scar—it was extraordinary. And when Shesepamuntayesher had looked at him, had knelt and stretched out a hand, as if she was a mother and he—

"Incredible, huh?" Professor Luben was beside him. Along with Officer Dover, they were the only ones left in the room. "Although I have to say, I'll be a bit relieved when she heads home tomorrow. I've been holding my breath for the past two days worrying that something might happen to her."

An image of his mother's cipher flashing in his brain, Cruz nodded.

"Cruz...I...uh...well, I'm not quite sure how to say this..." Cruz had never known Dr. Luben to be at a loss for words. "I wanted to say how sorry I am...about your dad's...disappearance."

Cruz dipped his head.

"Your aunt...she's concerned about you. She made me promise I'd keep her posted on how you were coping while she was away. And help out where I could."

Cruz looked up. "Really? 'Cause she made me promise the same thing about you. I'm supposed to tell her how things are really going in class—you know, without the cherry on top for her benefit."

Dr. Luben let out a laugh. "Looks like she's got us both reporting to her."

"Looks like."

His teacher studied him. "So how *are* you doing?"

"Hanging in there. You?"

"The same. But then my situation is far less difficult than yours." He slid his hands into his pockets. "If you ever need to talk to someone, I'm here..."

"Thanks." Naturally, he couldn't tell Dr. Luben about the cipher, Nebula, or the kidnapping, but he was grateful that his teacher cared. "I'll be okay."

"Spoken like a true explorer," said the professor. "Bucking up to the challenge is good, Cruz, but keeping things inside isn't."

"I know. I won't."

Professor Luben tipped his head. "You'd better get going. I'll text Monsieur Legrand and let him know I kept you late."

As he headed out of class, it occurred to Cruz that he really didn't know much about his professors, except for Aunt Marisol, of course. He'd picked up scraps of information about them here and there. He knew, for instance, that Professor Modi's wife was a teacher on board

Venture, one of the other Academy ships; that Professor Gabriel had a grandchild; and that Professor Benedict played blues guitar. It wasn't much. That's how it was with teachers, though, wasn't it? They knew far more about you than you did about them.

At the door, Cruz glanced back at Professor Luben, who was still admiring the sarcophagus. His teacher seemed to genuinely care about him. Then again, so had Mr. Rook and Tripp Scarlatos, and look how they had turned out.

Life would be so much easier if the bad guys were mean and the good guys were nice.

Seeing Cruz lingering at the door, his instructor nodded and smiled. Cruz returned the grin, lifted his hand, and hurried out of class.

8

►"YOU ALONE?"

"Yes," said Cruz to his best friend. "Emmett went…" He didn't know. "…somewhere."

Lani bent toward the camera. "I think I know where they're holding your dad."

The tablet fell from Cruz's fingers. He barely felt it smash his toes. *"What?"*

"Quiet," hushed his best friend, looking over her shoulder. "Your aunt is here."

Scooping his tablet off the floor of his cabin, Cruz collapsed into one of the overstuffed chairs. "Aunt Marisol…is with you?"

"She was going to stay at the St. Regis, but you know my mom."

That made sense. Cruz's cousins lived on the south end of the island, more than an hour's drive from Hanalei. Aunt Marisol would have booked a hotel room in Hanalei so she could be as close to home as possible.

"So what about my dad?" hissed Cruz. "How do you know where he is?"

"Okay, so Tiko and I went up to Limahuli yesterday. We drove around and spotted a house off Kuhio Highway next to the botanical gardens. I mean, it's *right* next door. If you were on the second floor looking out a window, you'd be able to see directly into the tiered gardens." Lani glanced over her shoulder again.

"That's it?" Cruz felt himself deflate. "You saw a house next to the botanical gardens?"

"If you'd let me finish, this was no ordinary house. It had a ten-foot concrete wall going all the way around it. The front gate had an *electrified* security system. And get this—the blinds were closed in *every* window. Even a celebrity on vacation is going to at least open the blinds to see the ocean view. I mean, that's why they come to Kauai, right? Plus, there were two big guys posted at the front door."

"You saw all that from the street?"

"Hardly. I climbed a banyan tree."

Of course she did.

"We didn't stay long, though," continued Lani. "It was getting dark. I'm telling you, Cruz, this *has* to be the place. Tiko's going to take me up again, and this time, I'm bringing some of my equipment."

"Lani, I don't think you should—"

"Are you kidding? It'll be the perfect chance to test out my acousticks."

Lani had been working on the water-filled tubes that amplified sound waves on and off for the past two years. She'd constructed them out of some kind of metamaterials—as usual, she wouldn't say what. Cruz often teased her that with her wizardry for inventing gadgets, she ought to become a professional spy. But this was no time for games.

"I'm not sure it's a good idea," he said. "If they catch you—"

"They won't. The acousticks have the range of a couple of football fields. I won't need to get anywhere near the house to hear everything they're saying inside. You don't have to worry, Cruz. I'm not about to do anything dumb or dangerous."

"I'm glad to hear it," said someone behind Lani.

Cruz knew that voice. *Aunt Marisol!*

His screen was suddenly a blur of hair as Lani whipped her head around. "Uh ... hi, Dr. Coronado. I ... um ... was telling Cruz that my uncle says I'm a good enough rider now to learn how to jump ... on a horse, I mean. I'm going to learn how to jump a horse. Yeah. Cruz was ... uh ... he was telling me to be careful."

"That's good advice," said Cruz's aunt. "Your mom's downstairs. She's ready to take you to school."

"Thanks. See ya later, Cruz. Don't worry. I won't fall off Stargazer." Her face zoomed close to the camera. She wiggled her eyebrows at him, before grabbing her backpack and trotting out of the room.

Aunt Marisol watched Lani go, then sat down in front of the laptop. "You doing okay?"

"Yeah," said Cruz. "Any news?"

"No." He could see the worry lines etched around her mouth and across her forehead. His aunt looked tired. "I spent most of yesterday with one of the detectives. They've done their best to retrace your dad's steps, but as far as anyone can tell, he was working at the Goofy Foot most of the day before he went missing. Several people saw him in the store, but no one noticed anything unusual. Your dad's sunglasses, a book he was reading, even his cup of coffee—were all still in the shop. It's like he suddenly disappeared off the face of the Earth. Poof!"

Cruz shivered. "What about our place over the shop?"

"The apartment was a little messy, but you know your father. He's not exactly tidy." She forced a grin. "The police say there's no sign of forced entry or a struggle, which is a relief. Still, they can't open a criminal investigation unless there's evidence of foul play. It looks like we're stuck for the moment. It's extremely frustrating."

Cruz's stomach was starting to churn. It was going to be harder than he'd expected, lying to her. On the helicopter pad, Cruz and Aunt Marisol had promised they wouldn't hide anything from each other, and here he was hiding *everything* from her. Cruz wanted to cry out, *It's Nebula! It's Nebula! They have Dad.* But he couldn't.

Aunt Marisol was glancing down, her face hidden by a curtain of hair. "Cruz, we said no secrets, right?"

The acid rose in his chest. He gulped it back down. "Right."

"I didn't want to say anything before I had all the facts, and I may be off base here, but"—she looked up—"I think Nebula may be behind this."

His throat burned. "N-Nebula?"

She bent toward him. "You must have wondered about it, too. I mean, they've been after you since before you entered the Academy. Didn't it ever cross your mind that they might try to use one of us to get to you and the cipher?"

"Well...y-yeah," he stuttered, his heart racing. "Sure, I...I...I wondered."

Smooth, Cruz. He had to get a grip or he'd blow the whole thing.

"I mean, vanishing without a trace?" Her dark eyes narrowed. "It's all too neat. This has Nebula written all over it, don't you think?"

A wave of panic rolled through him. Cruz didn't know what to say. If he said yes, he would be disobeying Nebula's orders, putting his father's life in danger. If he said no, he would be lying again and, worse, discouraging his aunt from pursuing what he knew to be true. His stomach was a burning knot. Grabbing his right elbow with his left hand and his left elbow with his right hand, Cruz pulled his forearms into his aching belly. "Uh... I don't know, Aunt Marisol."

"I'm sorry. I can see I've upset you. I didn't mean to—"

"It's all right. I'm fine, really." The last thing Cruz wanted to do was make her question telling him how she really felt. "I'm glad you said it, Aunt Marisol. Nebula is capable of anything and everything." Finally! A true statement. His stomach seemed to approve of his honesty. The pain began to ease, allowing Cruz to slightly release his hold.

"On the other hand, if it is Nebula, they should have contacted us by now with their demands, so maybe I'm on the wrong track." She rubbed the back of her neck. "I don't know."

Cruz longed to shout, *No! You're on the right track! Keep going!* Instead, he spoke the only truth he could. "You look like you haven't slept in a while."

"I haven't, but I will. Later. I thought I'd get an early start today so I can touch base with some of your dad's business contacts. I don't think his disappearance is work related, but it might give us a lead or two. Someone might know something or have seen something. How about you? How is anthro class going?"

"Great. We got to see a real sarcophagus and the ancient Egyptian woman who was buried in it, thanks to Fanchon's upgraded PANDA units. Now we're working on an assignment to find looting sites using satellite imagery."

"Space archaeology! Wonderful. How about Dr. Luben?"

"Everybody likes him. He's doing a good job—not as good as you, but close."

"And the journal? Have you figured out the third clue...?"

Bang! The cabin door smacked the back wall.

Cruz jumped. So did Aunt Marisol 7,000 miles away!

"That's it!" Emmett slammed the door as it bounced back to him. "I can't do it!" Tossing his tablet on his desk, he fell backward onto his bed. His glasses were dirt brown trapezoids. "I'm telling you, Cruz: I cannot. Do. It."

"Emmett?" Aunt Marisol was squinting. "What's wrong?"

Bolting up, Emmett spotted Aunt Marisol on Cruz's screen. "Uh... uh...uh..."

"It's one of Monsieur Legrand's survival training programs." Cruz rescued his sputtering roommate. "We're supposed to spend a couple of nights in the wilderness—well, the wilderness of the CAVE, anyway—and forage for food. Emmett's not a fan of bugs and worms."

"Right... that's it. Bugs. Ick." Emmett chewed on his lower lip. "No way, no how, am I eating those things."

Cruz rolled his eyes at his friend to say, *Don't overdo it.*

"I don't blame you," said Aunt Marisol. "Same here. Well, I'd better let you go. I've got work to do and it must be almost dinnertime there, huh? Talk soon." She kissed her fingertips, then put them close to the screen. "Love you, Cruz."

"Love you, too, Tía." Saying "auntie" in Spanish earned him a wide smile, which is why he said it.

"Sorry, sorry," burst Emmett the second Cruz ended the call. "I didn't realize you were talking to Dr. C or I would have—"

"Your timing was perfect. She was starting to ask about the next clue. If you hadn't barged in, I don't know what I would have said—definitely not the truth. So what's going on?"

"Your mom's journal." Emmett shook his head.

Cruz scooted across his bed to sit on the edge facing his friend. "That bad, huh?"

"Lani and I have done everything we can think to do. We analyzed the paper, hoping that might give us a clue, and it did help. We know it's a flexible material made of carbon polymer, tungsten trioxide, bamboo, and sunflowers. I tried exposing it to different things, being as safe as I could, hoping to trigger activation or some kind of reaction: hot and cold temps, water and air, sound and radio waves, and as many gases as possible without damaging the journal or blowing up the ship."

"And?"

"Nothing. It responded to nothing."

Cruz waited for Emmett to go on, but his roommate remained silent.

"So that's it?" squeaked Cruz. "You're giving up? I've never seen you give up on anything."

"And if this were one of *my* inventions I wouldn't," shot Emmett. "But this is your mom's journal. I don't want to destroy it."

"It's already broken. How much more could you do to it?"

"Plenty. As it is, someone who knows the technology might be able to fix it. But if I keep messing with it, I could expose it to the wrong thing and *boom*—there goes any chance you have of getting it to work again. *Ever.*"

Emmett was right. A broken journal was better than no journal at all. Wasn't it?

"Sorry, Cruz ... really sorry ..."

Cruz could see the stress on his friend's face. "I'm the one that should be saying I'm sorry, Emmett. It's not your fault. Lani and you did your best. Thanks for trying."

Emmett's pinched face relaxed a little, his glasses lightening to a honey brown. He opened his jacket pocket, took out the flat, digital journal, and handed it to Cruz.

Cruz ran his thumb along the outer edge of Lani's protective sleeve, then gently eased the white square paper from its gray case. Placing it on his left palm, he nudged it with his right index finger the way you do when you're a kid and have captured a grasshopper and want to feel it jump in your hand. Unlike an insect, the journal didn't move. No unfolding flaps. No multi-pointed sphere. No orange light. What had he expected, a miracle?

"There is someone," said Emmett. "She might—*might*—be able to fix it."

He meant Fanchon.

Cruz sighed. "I know you're right, but after what happened with Mr. Rook and Tripp…"

"I've been thinking about that." Emmett scooted to the edge of the bed, planted both feet on the floor, and looked Cruz directly in the eye. "You wouldn't have to tell her the whole story. You could say it's something your mom left for you—you know, like your holo-video at the beach. Fanchon would respect that. I know she would. We'll tell her we opened it once. That way we can explain how the activation sequence works, you know, how it goes from unfolding to transforming into the pointed sphere and then scans for identification. We'll say it got stuck when you tried to open it again. That should help her pinpoint the trouble. Plus, remember, the journal's content will only open for you, so even if she wanted to, she wouldn't be able to access any of the digital files."

"I don't know, Emmett." Cruz put a hand to his collar near his GPS Earth pin that would, with the tap of a finger, project an opaque holographic street map of any city in the world. Fanchon had designed everything the explorers wore, from their OS bands to their language translators. She'd invented Cruz's octopod and turned Emmett's Lumagine into their shadow badges, allowing them to transform the fabric of their uniforms using only the power of thought. She had even developed a helmet that could talk to whales! And that's exactly what scared him. Cruz glanced at the double-helix birthmark on his wrist. "If she knows how the technology operates, then wouldn't she know how to access the data, too? She might even be able to download it, and that *would* be a disaster. I really like Fanchon, and she is the smartest person I've ever known, but…"

"Okay, okay, fine," snapped Emmett. "I get it. She's nice. She's smart. She could help you. But you won't trust her."

"I can't. Don't you see, Emmett? I can't trust *anyone*. Not even kind, brilliant, helpful scientists."

"All right, if that's how you feel." He took off his glasses and set them on his nightstand. He headed for the bathroom. "I'll go wash up and we can go eat."

Cruz watched Emmett's frames slowly morph back to lime green ovals. He stared at the journal, still in his hand.

Cruz didn't know what to do. A few hours ago, Captain Iskandar had summoned Cruz to the bridge to find out if he had solved the next clue. They were sailing first to Spain, then to the mystery location somewhere in the Mediterranean that Aunt Marisol had told him about. Cruz had told the captain he needed to be in Istanbul, Turkey, by the morning of the 14th of November. However, he had neglected to mention why. Tomorrow they would be traveling through the Strait of Gibraltar, and two days after that the ship would dock at Barcelona. What if the next wedge of cipher was hidden *there*? Cruz would have no idea how to find it. More likely, it was hidden somewhere that they had passed already, like Norway, Scotland, or Ireland. For all Cruz knew, every nautical mile they traveled was taking him farther and farther away from the third piece of his mom's formula.

In her first journal entry, his mother had instructed him to let her recorded image know if he ever got stuck. Well, he was sure stuck now but had no way to reach her. He wished he could tell his aunt the truth. Or talk to his dad. One of them would know what to do. One of them would have the answers he did not. He felt so lost. So alone.

Cruz stared at the motionless page in his hand. That's what he needed, all right.

A miracle.

9

AFTER DINNER, Cruz went topside to the domed observatory at the stern of *Orion*'s bridge deck. It was one of his favorite places to go on the ship when he needed to do some serious thinking.

Stepping into the observatory was like stepping back in time. Old navigational charts covered most of the polished cherrywood-paneled walls. Between the maps, brass ship lanterns with red or green bulbs behind foggy ribbed glass swayed with the rhythm of the ship. Scattered about the room were all kinds of navigational instruments. You could peer through one of several telescopes or try your hand at using an antique sextant or astrolabe to calculate *Orion*'s position. The back corner had been converted into a greenhouse. Within the clear glass walls, solar-powered laser lights illuminated Chef Kristos's hydroponic garden of tomatoes, strawberries, lettuce, peppers, and other edibles. Potato and bean vines curled above the sprouting jungle, reaching for the warm, nurturing lights of the bubbled glass ceiling. The heavy scents of lavender, lemongrass, sage, dill, and rosemary filled the air.

No one was in the observatory when Cruz arrived. He supposed he should have been frightened that Nebula might corner him here, but he wasn't. He wouldn't let himself be. *Orion* was *his* ship, and Cruz refused to hide out in his cabin or give up his favorite thinking spot because of them. Emmett was right. Cruz could not give Nebula that kind of power over him. Still, his palms were slightly damp...

Settling into a soft maple-syrup-brown leather chair, Cruz looked to the east. In the distance, he could see the lights of the Portuguese coast. Cruz turned his gaze west, to watch the sun sink into the gray line of the ocean. Finally, he leaned his head back to stare up. Streamers of high, thin clouds dashed any hope of seeing the moon and stars.

Should he follow Emmett's advice? Should he let Fanchon Quills try to repair the journal? On their last explorer mission, someone had tampered with the Universal Cetacean Communicator rebreathing helmet Fanchon had designed, and Cruz had nearly drowned. After the incident, the horrified tech lab chief had insisted she would uncover the culprit. But she never had. On the other hand, Fanchon *had* devised the octopod for Cruz based on his mother's research. It seems unlikely she would have given him something to protect himself if she was working for Nebula. So the big question: Could he trust her?

His head still tilted up, Cruz saw a tiny glimmer of light. A single star. Then another and another, as the clouds above the ship began to evaporate. The Leonids would be starting in a few days. Cruz always looked forward to the annual meteor showers that began in early November and lasted through his birthday. Their geography and astronomy professor, Dr. Modi, was arranging things so the explorers could come up to the observatory after curfew and watch the meteor showers during their peak in the middle of the month. Cruz couldn't wait! The Leonids were pretty amazing to watch from land. Cruz had a feeling the fireballs would be even more spectacular to view from a ship.

Suddenly, Cruz felt something clamp on to his right elbow. *Nebula!* Snapping his head forward, he jerked away. He was about to throw a blind punch with his left hand, when a face popped around the side of the chair.

"Whatcha doing?"

"Sailor!" Cruz put a hand to his thumping heart.

Her ponytail swinging, she laughed. "Did I scare you?"

"Nah, I'm—"

"How about me?" Emmett sprung up from the left side of the chair.

Cruz jumped again. "Geez, you guys!"

"Sorry," chuckled Emmett.

Sailor glanced around. "What *are* you doing up here?"

"I don't know... hanging out."

"Got any plans for tonight?"

"Just homework."

"Ehhhhh!" She made a buzzer sound. "Wrong answer."

"You're coming with us." Emmett grabbed Cruz's left hand, while Sailor took his right. They pulled him out of his chair.

Cruz let out a laugh. "Do I have a choice?"

"Not really," said Sailor.

The pair led him out of the observatory.

"Can I at least know where we're going?" asked Cruz.

"Nope," answered Emmett. "You'll find out in a minute anyway." They walked him past the library, down the steps to the fourth deck, then one more flight to the third deck. When they reached the bottom of the stairs, Cruz saw that the lounge was filled with explorers. The chairs were lined up in rows and facing the big screen. Of course— movie night. He had forgotten.

"We thought it would help take your mind off things," whispered Sailor. "You need a break." At dinner, Emmett and Cruz had brought her up to speed on their progress, or lack of, concerning the journal.

Cruz wasn't exactly in the mood for a movie, but he supposed now that he was here, it would be rude to leave. Besides, the warm scent of fresh popcorn was hard to resist. Chef Kristos and Taryn were at a table near the entrance, handing out small bowls of flavored popcorn.

Along with the usual butter flavor, there was mac and cheese, eggs and bacon, and sugar cookie!

Taryn put a bowl into Cruz's hands. "You have to try the sugar cookie."

Cruz scooped up a few kernels coated in white chocolate and blue cupcake sprinkles. He popped them in his mouth. "Wow! It really does taste like cookies."

She grinned. "Secret family recipe."

"Chef Kristos let you in his galley?"

Taryn crossed her eyes. "Briefly."

Emmett had snagged three seats in the second-to-last row and was waving them over. Sailor scooted in to sit beside him, and Cruz took the seat at the end of the row. As the lights went down, Cruz checked around. "Isn't Bryndis coming?" he asked Sailor.

"She wanted to finish the looting tutorial. She was almost done when I left, so I think she might come up."

Cruz had completed their online tutorial that afternoon. In the training video, Professor Luben had explained that the satellite images they would be studying were taken nearly 400 miles above Earth. Each image was called a tile. He told them to look for circles or squares with rounded edges in the landscape because perfect circles or linear shapes, like squares or triangles, don't occur in nature. "Search for rectangles, too," he advised. "These are the places where looters may have encountered a feature, such as a wall or structure, and are moving along it. Also, looters don't just stop at one hole. They'll dig many. You're going to want to be on the lookout for groups of pits. The typical size of a pit is about five to sixteen feet across." Their instructor had told them to search for contrast within the surrounding landscape, and had said that sometimes, when the sun was at the right angle, the looting pits would cast shadows.

"One other thing," Dr. Luben had said. "In class, remember how we discussed that looters will sometimes use heavy machinery to dig pits? Keep your eyes open for any large disturbances in the landscape, like the parallel tracks from a bulldozer. A database of tiles from your assigned countries will be waiting for you in the library at your scheduled time. Please review the images and flag those that appear to have pits. Take your time. There's no rush. Don't get discouraged if it takes you a while to tell the difference between a bush and a pit. This type of work takes practice, which is why as soon as I get done jabbering you'll get to do a practice round of tiles. This is not a test. False positives are going to happen, and it's better to flag a tile if you aren't sure than to let it go. The experts can take a look and make the final call." He'd leaned in. "By the way, a bush is fuzzier, less defined, and usually a different color than a pit. Good luck, explorers!"

Cruz had done well on his practice round. He'd gotten 18 of the 20 tiles correct. Team Cousteau was scheduled to do the real thing in the library tomorrow at 5 p.m. Even though Professor Luben had insisted it wasn't a test, it was. It might not be graded, but the explorers knew what was at stake. If there was looting going on, it was their job to find it.

The sound of a rocket engine shook Cruz back to reality. The movie was about space explorers battling aliens who were trying to go back in time to the early 21st century and change Earth's history. Or was it the humans who were trying to go back in time? Cruz wasn't sure. It was hard to focus. Plus, he wasn't a big fan of space-time continuum story lines anyway. Too convoluted. Too convenient. Too silly. Munching down the last of his sugar-cookie popcorn, he looked around the darkened lounge. A few feet behind him, Taryn was kneeling. She snapped a leash on to her dog's collar.

Cruz stretched over the arm of his chair. "I'll walk Hubbard for you," he whispered.

"Don't you want to see the rest of the movie?"

"I'd rather take Hub for his walk."

"Okay, then."

Cruz tapped Sailor's shoulder. "Be back in a while."

"Uh-huh." She didn't take her eyes off the screen.

Cruz crept over to Taryn.

She handed him the leash. "He might have to use his personal meadow."

Hubbard had his own patch of grass on the outdoor stern deck just off the passage next to Cruz and Emmett's cabin.

"We'll go there first," said Cruz.

Taryn also gave him Hubbard's favorite green ball. "Thanks, Cruz."

He gave her a quick wave. For having such little legs, the white Westie sure was speedy. Hubbard galloped to the stairs, then flew down them, with Cruz doing his best to keep up. At the bottom of the grand staircase, Hubbard took a sharp left and trotted down the explorers' passage straight to the back door to the sundeck.

Cruz snickered. "You know the way, Hub, don't you?"

When Hubbard had finished in his meadow, Cruz took him back inside. They played a few rounds of fetch in the explorers' passage. Cruz refilled the water bowl Taryn kept for Hubbard in the hallway. While the pup slurped water, Cruz did a quick check of Hubbard's yellow life vest to make sure he was still in possession of the cipher pieces. He was. At least *something* was going the way he'd planned.

Cruz was on one knee, putting Hubbard's leash back on, when the door to Sailor and Bryndis's cabin opened.

Bryndis stepped out, her laundry bag slung over one shoulder. "Hi."

"Hi. How'd the tutorial go?"

"Eighteen out of twenty."

"Me too," he said.

"You didn't go to the movie either?"

"I did, but I left to walk Hubbard for Taryn." He squished his nose. "Space-time continuum plot."

She gave him a sympathy groan, then nodded to her bag. "Droppin' off. Want to walk Hubbard in my direction?"

Cruz got to his feet. "Sure, if you don't mind."

"Yes. I mean, no, I don't mind." Pale cheeks turned pink.

They headed across the atrium to the stairs and went down a flight to the main deck. A left turn would have taken them aft to the CAVE.

Bryndis, Cruz, and Hubbard swung right, heading forward through housekeeping to laundry. Bryndis handed her bag over the desk to the crewman on duty. They retraced their steps, but Hubbard made it difficult. He started to bounce between them.

"I think he wants to play," said Bryndis, gesturing to the ball in Cruz's hand.

Cruz unhooked the dog's leash. He tossed the ball down the narrow passage toward the CAVE. Hubbard bolted after it. Cruz and Bryndis slowly followed.

Cruz peered ahead. "I've never been past the CAVE."

"There's not much to see on this deck." Bryndis pointed. "Some of the crew's quarters are up ahead and beyond that is galley storage and refrigeration. There's also a small repair shop at the stern."

"How do you know all this? Did you memorize the ship's layout or something?"

"No." She grinned, a dimple appearing on each side of her mouth. "I run."

"You run? On the ship?"

"Uh-huh. If you go early in the morning, there's hardly anyone up then. I can pretty much go anywhere I want. That's how I know it so well. I've seen it from top to bottom, bow to stern. Well, most of it." She twisted her lips. "There is *one* door . . ."

He glanced at her. "What?"

"It's a plain door with no sign or anything. It has a sensor security lock, but when I hold my OS band up to it nothing happens."

They both knew what that meant: The area was off-limits to explorers.

Hubbard was charging straight for them with his ball. Skidding to a stop, he dropped it at Cruz's feet. Bending, Cruz threw it again. "That's strange," he said, watching Hubbard race down the passage. "I didn't know there was someplace on the ship we couldn't go. I mean, I know we're supposed to ask for permission to be on the bridge and the helicopter pad, but I didn't know there was an area that was completely restricted."

"Me either."

Could it be true? Did *Orion* have a secret compartment? And if so, why?

"It's one deck down." Bryndis raised an eyebrow. "Want to see?"

Did he?

When Hubbard returned, Cruz scooped up the ball and snapped on his leash. They headed down the stairs to B deck. Cruz had been to the lowest level of *Orion* many times. It was where the control room, also known as the engine room, was located, along with aquatics, where all of their scuba gear was stored. It was also home to *Ridley*, the ship's mini submarine. Every Sunday since he'd come on board, Cruz had eagerly zipped down these steps to the aquatics room, where chief Tripp Scarlatos had been teaching him how to pilot the sub—that is, until recently. Cruz had not been back to this part of the ship since Tripp and Security Officer Wardicorn had attempted to bury Team Cousteau in an ice cave collapse in Iceland. The two men had been secretly working for Nebula, just waiting for their chance to get rid of Cruz. Now Cruz missed his pilot training, and although he knew he shouldn't, he also missed Tripp. It had been fun, learning to be a sub pilot. Before she left, Aunt Marisol had told him Dr. Hightower was going to hire a new aquatics director. Cruz was excited about the prospect. And if he was honest, a bit scared.

Bryndis started toward aquatics but veered left off the main passage before she reached the turn. Cruz and Hubbard stayed on her tail. This part of the ship was a bit of a maze, with narrow corridors and tight corners. It was also not well lit. They made several turns before the passage ended at a sapphire blue door with no handle. Just as Bryndis had said, a black security screen was attached to the wall next to the unmarked door. Cruz held his OS band up to it.

"See?" sighed Bryndis, after several seconds.

Cruz didn't see any surveillance equipment. "If this was a top secret room, they'd have cameras and tighter security."

"*Já*, it's probably a locked cargo hold, you know, with stuff inside that they don't want anyone getting into."

"It could be a lounge for the crew or professors," offered Cruz.

"Of course." Bryndis planted a palm on her forehead. "Like the faculty room back at the Academy. I'll bet that's what it is. No wonder *we* can't get in."

Out of all the scenarios, that did seem to make the most sense.

Letting out a whine, Hubbard pulled on his leash. "He's ready to go," said Cruz. As Bryndis turned away, Cruz stopped her. "Wait!"

He had an idea.

"I know a way we might be able to solve the mystery."

She tipped her light blond head. "How?"

Cruz opened his lower right pocket. "Mell, on."

"Good ole Mell to the rescue!" cried Bryndis.

"Mell, fly to the doorframe and remain there until I recall you," instructed Cruz. "If anyone comes in or out of the blue door, record it, and send the video immediately to my tablet with an alert. Stealth mode, on. Confirm, please."

The honeybee drone flashed her golden eyes to indicate she understood.

Bryndis tipped her head. "Stealth mode?"

"It means she isn't to engage anyone or get close enough for them to see her." Cruz gave the "go" command, and Mell flew up to land on the ledge of the doorjamb. She moved her tiny striped body to face outward, then scooted back until she was out of sight. He turned to Bryndis. "We should get topside or Taryn will start to wonder where—"

The communications pin on his jacket crackled. "Taryn to Cruz Coronado."

Bryndis put a hand to her mouth to stifle her laughter, while Cruz assured their adviser he was on his way back to the lounge.

"Can I walk Hubbard back up?" asked Bryndis.

"Yeah, but it's more like the other way around. *He* walks you. Don't let his size fool you." Cruz handed her the leash.

As Cruz had warned, Hubbard set their return at a brisk pace. Funny how the dog seemed to know the way out of the maze. He didn't miss a single turn. Was he following their original scent? Or had he been here before? Maybe Taryn had brought him. Cruz doubted the bright blue door was hiding anything important. Still, it would be fun trying to unlock the mystery with Bryndis. Hubbard slowed once they reached the main passage.

"Cruz, I've been meaning to ask you," said Bryndis. "I thought you might tell me ... you know, when you were ready, but ..." Her voice trailed off.

He had been expecting this. Back in Iceland, Cruz, Sailor, Emmett, and Bryndis had nearly lost their lives when Tripp and Officer Wardicorn had set off the explosive in the ice cave. There, Bryndis learned that the two men were working for Nebula and were after the journal that had belonged to Cruz's mom, but she didn't know why they wanted it. She'd also, of course, been there when Cruz had found the second wedge of his mother's cipher but again had no clue as to what it was. Cruz had promised to fill her in on the details once they'd returned to

the ship, yet he hadn't. He was having second thoughts. The fewer people who knew his secret, the better. For everyone.

Still, he had made a promise. Cruz knew he would have to choose his
words carefully.

"Tripp and Wardicorn were working for Nebula, the drug company,"
he began. "They wanted my mom's digital journal because they thought
it contained some scientific information that could help their company."

"Does it?"

"Maybe. I haven't seen the whole thing."

One lie. One truth. Not bad.

"And the stones?"

"Those go to a . . ." Cruz hesitated. He didn't want to use the word
"cipher." " . . . a puzzle."

"A puzzle?" She tipped her head. "You mean, it's a game?"

"S-sort of." This was getting more complicated by the second. "Actually, it's more like a . . . a gift. My mom left these stones in different
places around the world for me to discover. They're no big deal—little
pieces she laser-cut to fit together like a puzzle. So that's what I was—
am—doing. As we travel, I'm finding the stones my mom left."

"How do you know where to look?"

"She left clues, too," said Cruz. "I know it sounds weird, but it's what
we do in my family. Before I came to the Academy, Aunt Marisol used to
send me postcards to decode from wherever she was in the world. Just
before we set sail on *Orion,* I found out my mom did something similar before she died. My dad said she hoped that one day I might go to
Explorer Academy and it would be . . . fun for me to discover them."

"I think I see. It's like a *minningarhátíð* . . . I'm not sure of the
English word for it . . . something that's left behind from one you love
with a *minni* . . . you know . . . a memory."

"You mean, a keepsake?" Cruz let out a ragged breath. "That's what
it is, a keepsake."

Was this conversation over yet?

Cruz nearly tripped over Hubbard, who had abruptly stopped at the bottom of the grand staircase in the atrium. The third-floor lounge above them was still dark. They could hear the movie's audio—laser blasts and loud music.

Bryndis put Hubbard's leash in Cruz's hand, brushing his fingers with hers. "Thanks."

He felt a tiny shock go through him. Static, probably. "Anytime."

Leaning in, Bryndis gave him a kiss on the cheek. It was so quick and light, for a moment Cruz wondered if he had imagined it. Turning, she strolled away down the explorers' passage. She did not look back, but when she turned to open her cabin door, he caught a glimpse of her face.

Bryndis was smiling.

So was he.

10

HAD SOMEONE called his name? Cruz was standing on a narrow red clay path, surrounded on all sides by a tropical jungle. The air was thick and hot. This path, these trees, the red dust under his feet—it all seemed familiar, but he couldn't think where—

"Cruz!"

His heart lurched. "Dad?" Cruz spun, the forest becoming a green blur. "Where are you?"

"Here! I'm over here!"

"Hold on!" cried Cruz. He took off running on the trail in the direction of the cry. His dad seemed to be only a few hundred yards ahead, yet when Cruz rounded the next bend, there was no sign of him. He cupped his hands around his mouth. "Dad?"

Someone was shaking him. "Cruz? Cruz, wake up!" The face that appeared in front of him wasn't his father's. It was Emmett's.

"What's wrong?" croaked Cruz, still trying to separate the dream from reality.

"Your tablet's been chiming. You've got a call..."

"From Aunt Marisol?"

"No. It's Lani." Emmett held out Cruz's tablet to him.

Sitting up, he squinted against the light of the screen. "Lani?"

"Sorry to wake you." She was whispering. "I thought you'd want to see this."

"That's okay." He yawned. "What's up?"

"Hold on," she hissed. "I have to backtrack—"

He couldn't see past her. "Where are you?"

"Inside the house."

Cruz bolted upright. "Not the one in—"

"Yes, yes, the house next to Limahuli gardens. I got in!"

"Lani, get out of there!" He was wide awake now. "You're going to get caught—"

"No, I won't. Tiko and I staked out the place for almost an hour before I went over the wall. Staked? Is that the right word? Stuck? Anyway, Tiko's right outside. He'll let me know if anyone's coming."

"Did she say over the wall?" asked Emmett.

Cruz's blood was beginning to boil. As it was, he was worried to death about his dad. He didn't need to add Lani to that list. "She's going to get herself killed."

"I am not," shot Lani. "I did full surveillance. My acousticks and heat sensors picked up nothing, not even so much as a mouse, although I did find something interesting once I got in. I'm switching you over to my headset cam."

Moments later he was looking at the toes of Lani's red striped sneakers on a plush ivory carpet. Lani tilted the camera up. It was a bedroom. She turned her head slowly so they could see the moss green walls, a large but simple four-poster bed with a white quilt, and a rattan nightstand and matching dresser. As she continued panning, Cruz saw a couple of French doors that led to a balcony and two more interior doors—the bathroom and a closet, no doubt. The camera began to bounce. Lani was heading across the room to the second door. As she entered, Cruz saw shelves and rails. Yep, it was a closet, all right. The place was completely empty, except for a few hangers. Lani tipped her head to show them rows of wire shoe racks without a single shoe.

"Big walk-in," murmured Emmett, twisting his neck to get a better view of Cruz's screen.

Lani was still in motion. She went past an upright oval mirror, a wall unit with long wood drawers, and a half wall of square cubbies. She turned, and Cruz saw a white kitchen chair with a rounded, spindled back. Clearly out of place, it set the hair on the back of Cruz's neck standing on end. Lani knelt next to the chair. "I found these," she said, lifting a couple of ropes tied to the spokes. Cruz could see there were more ropes tied to the white legs.

His breath caught.

"And this," continued Lani. She flipped the chair. "I saw an end of it hanging down—"

"Dad's bracelet!" Goose bumps slithered up his arms.

An identical bracelet circled Cruz's right wrist. Aunt Marisol had given them the red-and-green beaded dragon bracelets for their birthdays last year. Cruz's dad's birthday was December 1, just two days after his. Like Cruz, his father always wore his bracelet. Always. He would never leave it behind unless he had to. It was a clear message from his dad: *I was here.*

"It looks like he stuck it on here with some grape jelly. Pretty smart." Lani peeled the bracelet away from the wood. "I'm sorry, Cruz. I should have called the police yesterday when we saw this place. We could have rescued him—"

"Or gotten him killed," cut in Cruz. "You did the right thing by staying away, Lani. If we're going to get Dad back safely, we've got to follow Nebula's instructions."

The camera went slowly up and down to signal she was in agreement.

"Lani, two favors?" asked Cruz.

"Name 'em."

"Don't show my aunt the bracelet."

"I won't," she said softly. "And the second?"

"Get out of that house. Now."

"On my way." She headed back through the closet and into the bedroom. "Okay, guys, I'm going to say goodbye."

"Lani, wait!" burst Emmett, his glasses yellow triangles with blue and green sparks.

"What?"

"There's something on the floor by your feet. I saw it when you first turned on the headset cam. It's pink. Do you see it?"

"No, I don't … Oh, you mean this?" She knelt. "It's a piece of paper … it looks like it's a corner from a salt or sugar packet." She held it up to the lens. "There's something else …"

The camera whirled around, then zoomed in. They watched her fingers comb the carpet. She brought a hand up. "It's definitely sugar," said Lani. "And it's all through the carpet here. Someone must have spilled it by accident."

"Or on purpose," said Emmett.

Cruz's pulse quickened. Was it possible? Had his dad left another clue?

"Why would anyone dump sugar all over—" Lani let out a gasp. "Oh my gosh! Of course: Koloa! It has to be Koloa." The view from the camera looked like an earthquake had hit, as she rushed into the hallway. "I'm on it, Cruz! Don't worry. I'll find him."

"No!" he yelled. "It's too risky."

"I'll call you when I can get there," she huffed. "It'll take me a few days to work it out, though. Aloha."

"Lani, don't do it!" shouted Cruz. "Don't go. Do. Not. Go. Did you hear me? Lani? *Lani?*"

The screen was black. Cruz slapped the bed.

"Where's she going?" asked Emmett.

"To an abandoned sugar mill. Koloa is on the south end of the island. I don't like this. The last thing we need is for Nebula to discover she's following them."

"I'm sure Lani wouldn't do anything crazy."

"Really? 'Cause I'm not." Cruz grabbed his phone off the nightstand and began texting her as fast as his fingers could fly. "You don't know her like I do. Once she's committed to something, she can get a little carried away. Who am I kidding? She can get *a lot* carried away. Lani Kealoha is the most stubborn, hardheaded, unreasonable girl I've ever met in my life ..." Pausing, Cruz glanced up. "And if anything ever happened to her ..."

"It won't. She'll be all right. You'll see." Emmett's words would have been a lot more convincing if his glasses weren't gray crescent moons of fear.

"WHAT ABOUT THAT SPOT in the southwest corner?" Sailor pointed diagonally across the screen beneath her hand.

It was late afternoon, and Team Cousteau was huddled around one of the computerized map tables in the library. They were working on Professor Luben's looting assignment. As instructed, they were reviewing satellite tiles from Turkey and flagging those that appeared to have looting pits.

"I don't think it's a pit," said Emmett. "There's only one hole. Remember, Dr. Luben said looters rarely stop with one hole."

Sailor nodded. "Cruz, what do you think?"

"Huh?" Cruz was going between the screens on his tablet and phone. He had been calling and texting Lani all day. She wasn't responding.

"The tile?" Sailor sounded annoyed. "Is the spot in the corner a pit or not?"

Cruz stretched toward her.

"Try looking in the right place, Coronado." Dugan, who was to the left of Cruz, tapped the screen between them.

"Sorry." Cruz shifted his gaze.

After a few seconds, Dugan nudged Bryndis, who was at the controls. "Let's go on to the next one."

"Not yet," she answered calmly.

"Why not? Three out of the five of us don't see anything."

"We agreed that we *all* have to agree on each tile," said Bryndis.

"I didn't agree to Coronado going slower than a sloth," said Dugan.

"If we go too fast, we could miss something," said Emmett.

Dugan grunted. "Yeah, like dinner."

"No one is missing dinner," Bryndis said evenly. "We're almost done with this one."

"I'm done." Cruz lifted his head.

Bryndis giggled. "See?"

Dugan rolled his eyes, but he grinned, too.

Cruz admired the way Bryndis handled Dugan during their team projects. She was cool but firm. She also didn't seem to let Dugan's doom-and-gloom attitude affect her. Dugan's bleak outlook had a way of sticking to you without you realizing it, kind of like syrup when you're eating pancakes.

"I would say no pit," said Cruz. "Emmett's right. Plus, remember the tutorial said that in order to gauge the size of the hole we should compare it to landmarks on the tile, like cars or houses. It's twice the size of that building near Dugan's elbow. It's too big to be a pit."

"Good," said Sailor. "That's five no votes for Tile Twenty-Two."

Bryndis entered it into the computer. "How about if we do one more? That leaves seven tiles, and we can finish them tomorrow."

Everyone nodded.

Tile 23 came up. Cruz bent to scan his side of the satellite image. He was improving as they went along. Cruz was getting better at telling the difference between trees and bushes, hills and divots, even farms and random bulldozer tracks. The image had mostly flat brown plains with a few wrinkled hills broken up by rocky outcrops. To his right, in the southeast corner, Cruz could make out dozens of dark circles in a grid pattern. Looting pits. But there was something else, too—something he had not seen before. Beneath the dirt, he could see the faint outline of three large rings, one inside the other. It was like looking at a lopsided wedding cake from above. In the center ring were two small squares sitting corner to corner. If this was a historic site preserved by archaeologists, it should have been labeled on the tile. Maybe it was an archaeological feature, a site that looters had partially uncovered but that had not been properly unearthed by scientists.

"Dugan," Cruz said to the bent head next to his. "What do you think this is?"

His teammate slid over. Lines wriggled across his forehead as he inspected the landscape. "I don't know. Probably an archaeological feature."

"That's what I thought, too, but what *is* it?"

"No clue. Like it matters. We're supposed to be looking for pits."

"Yeah, I know, but aren't you curious?"

"About what?" asked Sailor.

Cruz motioned to the rest of the team. Everyone scooted around to Dugan and Cruz's side of the square table.

"Whatever it is, those circles have to be human-made," said Bryndis.

"It could be a temple," said Sailor.

"Or a tomb," suggested Emmett.

They studied the image for several more minutes, but none of them knew what to make of the faint outlines.

"I'll make a note for Professor Luben," said Bryndis, moving to the touch-screen keyboard. "I bet he'll know what it is. Does anyone have any looting pits to report?"

Cruz lifted his hand. "I do."

Dugan and Emmett chimed in that they did, too. Once every member of Team Cousteau had studied every other member's sections and they'd all agreed, Bryndis added those sites to her notes as well. "I'm scheduling us for map time tomorrow at three p.m., right after class lets out," she said. "Let's go eat. It's build-your-own-mini-pizza night."

"I'm so hungry I could eat three," said Dugan.

"Same here." Emmett shot Cruz a grin. "Pepperoni and sausage with extra cheese?"

"Actually, I thought I'd stick around here for a little longer," said Cruz. "I ... uh ... I need to study for Modi's geography test."

"Hardly." Sailor smirked. "I graded your practice quiz. You didn't miss a single question, not even that one about how far Russia is from America."

Bryndis groaned. "I can't believe I missed that."

"I got it right," said Dugan.

Everyone began chattering about how Professor Modi had thrown a trick question at them: In the Bering Strait, the island of Big Diomede belonged to Russia, and nearby Little Diomede was part of Alaska, meaning the countries were just a little over two miles apart! While his teammates were busy talking, Cruz took the opportunity to grab his tablet and slip into the stacks. He headed to the aft section of the library, trotting up the spiral staircase to the second floor.

Cruz had work to do. He had decided to try to fix the holo-journal himself. It wasn't that he didn't believe Emmett or Lani when they'd said they had tried everything, but they'd also been wary about breaking his mom's journal. Maybe they had been too careful, had given up too soon.

Cruz pulled up the library's database on his tablet and did a search for books on computational origami, materials architecture, and holo-technology. On-screen, the opposite corner of the second-floor library diagram lit up. It activated the GPS pin on Cruz's collar, projecting a line of opaque blue dots in front of him. They would take him to the section where the books were shelved. He began following the polka dots. Through rails of the balcony, Cruz saw Team Magellan below him. Ali, Matteo, Yulia, Kat, Tao, and Zane were just entering the library. It was a few minutes after six.

They'd probably already eaten and were now coming at their scheduled time to do their tiles for anthropology class. Cruz noticed that while Sailor, Bryndis, and Emmett headed past the other explorers and out the door, Dugan hung back. He said something to Matteo, throwing out an arm in the direction of the map tables. Matteo laughed. Instead of following the rest of his team out of the library, Dugan leaned backward, as if checking to be certain his teammates had left, then followed Team Magellan to a map table. So much for being hungry enough to eat a few mini pizzas. Could Emmett be right about their teammate?

"Just what are you up to, Dugan Marsh?" muttered Cruz.

When Dugan disappeared, Cruz continued on his way, following the line of hovering blue dots to the section on holo-technology. Settling into one of the closed-off study nooks, Cruz spent the next two hours going through a short stack of thick books. He studied the principles of computational origami, how paper and other materials are folded via computer program. He learned about the science behind materials architecture, the ways in which different materials change in response to stimuli and their environment. Cruz had seen self-assembling furniture and self-driving cars, but now he was beginning to understand how these things worked. It was exciting stuff. This must have been how Emmett had felt when he was researching how to create his mind-control fabric, Lumagine.

In his reading, Cruz also stumbled upon why his mother had used tungsten trioxide to make her journal. The compound's ability to regulate heat and light made it fire retardant and resistant to sun damage. Still, there was a great deal of information that was beyond him. Most of the books dealt with current hardware. Something seven years old was considered ancient. Plus, the math was too advanced.

His neck cramping and his stomach rumbling, Cruz slammed shut the cover of the last book in his pile. He *did* understand more about the technology but, sadly, not enough to fix the journal.

Cruz slid open the door to the nook and stuck out his head. The aisle was empty. Scooping up his books, Cruz scurried out to reshelve them before he was spotted. His heart pounded as he shoved each title into place. Pushing in the last spine, Cruz spun on his heel and walked straight into Sidril Vanderwick. He heard her toes crunch beneath his.

"I'm sorry, Dr. Vanderwick," said Cruz. "Are you okay?"

The science tech lab assistant hopped on one foot. "Uh-huh. What are pinkie toes really good for anyway?" The corners of her mouth turned up.

Cruz couldn't recall ever seeing Dr. Vanderwick smile. Not that he ever saw much of Fanchon's second-in-command. Whenever he went to the lab, Dr. Vanderwick was usually busy in one of the cubicles working on an experiment or in one of the back labs. She was quite different from Fanchon. Where the tech lab chief was a churning tornado of colorful clothes and wild hair and mind-blowing ideas coming at you at 100 miles an hour, Dr. Vanderwick was more like a soft breeze. She wore a white lab coat over a dark turtleneck and a skirt or pants. Her honey blond hair was usually pulled away from her face into a tight bun or ponytail. He knew she was extremely bright, too. More than once Cruz had heard the lab chief say she would be lost without her assistant.

Moving past him, Dr. Vanderwick reached for one of the books Cruz had put back on the shelf a half minute earlier. He tried not to look guilty. He didn't need to worry. The scientist was busy looking up something in the index. She flipped back through several chapters, found the page she needed, and read a few paragraphs. "Ah, of course!"

"You've studied holography?" Cruz gulped.

"A little." Shutting the book, she turned it around so Cruz could see the cover.

It had her name on it. It was his turn to gasp. "*You* wrote this?"

Another grin.

Cruz couldn't believe it. Maybe Emmett was right. If they ever hoped to get the journal working again, Cruz would have to trust *someone* with expertise in the technology. And here she was, standing right in front of him. It was a . . . a . . .

Miracle.

Sort of. Fanchon was likely an expert, too, but Dr. V hadn't designed a helmet that had nearly killed him.

No one else was around. If Cruz was going to ask for her help, it was the perfect time.

"Dr. Vanderwick?" Taking a deep breath, Cruz reached inside the lower outside pocket of his uniform. His fingers slid over his mom's journal. "I was wondering . . . I thought maybe . . . you could help me with something."

"Sure. If I can."

"I've got this—"

Laughter interrupted him. "…and then I got so freaked out at seeing a snake, I jumped up and took off running as fast as I could," crowed a deep voice from below, "and fell right into the latrine hole."

More laughter.

Cruz didn't need to go to the rail to find out who it was, but he did anyway. He couldn't resist. Professor Luben was standing at one of the map tables. Team Magellan was clustered around him, hanging on his every word. "And that deadly horned viper?" boomed their instructor. "It turned out to be a piece of rubber from an old tire."

The explorers howled.

Snickering, Cruz turned back to Dr. Vanderwick. "It's only Professor Lu—"

But she was gone. Guess Dr. Vanderwick was in a hurry to return to the lab. Cruz wondered, should he follow her and try again to ask if she would help repair the journal? Maybe it wasn't such a good idea after all. In order to fix the digital book, she'd need to keep it for a while, and he wasn't sure he wanted to part with it for any length of time. Plus, she might tell others she had it, including Fanchon.

Cruz put a hand through his hair, pulling it up by the roots until he tipped his own head back. He was looking at the beautiful stained-glass map of the world on the ceiling. In the dimming light of evening, he could not make out the tiny Hawaiian Islands in the vast, swirling blue of the Pacific Ocean. He felt restless.

What should he do?

Cruz's tablet was chiming. It had to be Lani. It was about time, too. He'd sent at least a dozen texts. Lowering his head, he tapped the icon, but the message wasn't from Lani. It was from Mell. She had recorded someone near the secret door!

Cruz hit the "play" arrow, his pulse quickening. The video began with Mell zooming in on the approaching figure. However, the drone was compensating for the dim light in the passage by widening her aperture, even as she tried to focus in on a moving target. The poor light and jerky movement made it impossible to tell who was coming down the corridor. Just when Mell managed to bump up the light level and bring things into focus, the person leaned into the security camera for identification, and Cruz was stuck looking at the top of a head. Hearing the door unlock, Cruz let out a moan. Great. He wasn't going to be able to ID the mystery guest.

The figure took a step back. Cruz held his breath. As the blue door opened, a cone of light appeared from the secret room. It illuminated a face that Cruz had never in a million years expected to see!

11

"JERICHO MILES?" Emmett

froze in the doorway of the bathroom, toothpaste foaming from his mouth. "On this ship? You saw Jericho Miles on board *Orion*?"

"I didn't, but Mell did." Cruz held up his tablet. "I've got the video to prove it."

"One sec." Emmett ran to spit out his toothpaste. He was back in a flash.

Cruz played the drone footage for his roommate. The gaunt face, the long blond ponytail, the lean runner's body—there could be no doubt this was the scientist who had saved Cruz, Emmett, and Sailor back at the Academy from Nebula's gas attack. After rescuing them, Jericho had brought the trio inside the top secret lab. He wouldn't admit that's where they were, but Emmett had figured it out, based on the security features and a few other clues. Later, Jericho had shown up again, this time at the Society's museum, to save Cruz from one of Nebula's hit men. Even so, Jericho had been on a mission, too. The Synthesis had sent him to the museum to get a blood sample from Cruz. Jericho wouldn't say why and, in fact, claimed not to know, but Cruz wasn't so sure about that. In the end, Jericho had let Cruz off the hook. He had released him without ever getting the sample. Even so, when it came to Jericho Miles, Cruz had far more questions than answers.

The pair watched the Synthesis scientist pass through the blue door. When Mell's video went to black, Emmett turned to Cruz. "What's *he* doing *here*?"

Cruz shrugged. "I wish I knew."

In her journal, Cruz's mother had warned him about the Synthesis. She'd said she could no longer be certain that the very organization that she had helped originate was on her side. With no one left to trust, she had created and hidden the cipher with her formula for Cruz—and only Cruz—to find. At first, Cruz had found it hard to believe that the Synthesis might turn on his mom, but now he was beginning to understand her misgivings. Since his arrival at the Academy, Cruz had not come any closer to learning whether the Synthesis was an ally or an enemy. And as long as it remained a mystery, he had to be careful.

"It's possible Jericho might not even be here for you," said Emmett. "In fact, now that I think about it, it makes perfect sense he'd be hiding in the belly of the ship."

Cruz's eyes widened. "It does?"

"Can you think of a better way for a *top secret* branch of the Society dedicated to studying the potential of humankind to investigate new discoveries made around the world?"

Cruz saw his point. Traveling with a ship full of explorers *would* be good cover. Maybe Jericho's presence here had absolutely nothing to do with him.

"Still..." Emmett frowned. "Maybe you ought to steer clear of B deck and let Mell keep an eye on things there for a while. Just to be safe."

"Jericho Miles doesn't scare me," scoffed Cruz. It wasn't true, of course. "But if you think it's a good idea..."

Someone was knocking on the door. Cruz opened it to a worried-looking Sailor. He stepped back, and she quietly marched past him. However, the moment the door was closed, she burst, "If you're mad at me, just say it. I can take that. I hate the silent treatment."

"Mad? Why would I be mad?"

"Back in the library, you wouldn't come with us to dinner. And then you gave that lame excuse about studying for our geo unit test. I was sure you were angry with me for telling you to pay attention to the tiles."

"I'm not mad, Sailor."

Her frown softened. "Are you crook?"

"Crook?"

"You know ... sick. How do you Americans say it? Tossing your biscuits?"

"Cookies," corrected Cruz's Canadian roommate.

"Biscuits, cookies, whatever."

"No," said Cruz with a chuckle. "Not crook either."

"So you really did want to study?"

A shadow crossed his face. It was only for a second, but Sailor saw it before he could mask it and pounced. "I knew it. Something *is* going on." Her lips formed a line of determination.

"I ... I couldn't say anything with Bryndis and Dugan standing there," explained Cruz. "I wanted to see ... I mean, I thought maybe if ..." He let out a long sigh. No matter how delicately he put this, he was going to hurt Emmett's feelings. "When you said you couldn't fix the journal, Emmett, it's not that I didn't think Lani and you didn't know what you were doing, but I ... well, I guess I needed to understand for myself why it was hopeless. I needed to be sure there wasn't any-thing I could do. Know what I mean?"

"Uh-huh," said Emmett, but he still looked hurt. "And are you ... sure now?"

"Yes. You were right. Although while I was there I saw Dr. Vanderwick. Did you know she's an expert on holography? She wrote a book about it."

"She did? What's the title?"

"Um ... something about the basics and principles of holography, or maybe it was the science and practice of holography. Search her name and you'll find it—"

"Whoa!" Sailor stepped between them. "Back up a minute. Are you both positive you can't fix the journal? What did you try?"

"What didn't we?" answered Emmett. "The journal's made from bamboo and sunflower in a carbon polymer base, so we exposed it to everything we thought might spark the activation process: sound waves, radio waves, heat, cold..."

"And?"

"Nothing."

Putting her hands on her hips, Sailor shuffled toward the door to the veranda. Emmett took a seat at his desk. He began typing on one of his three computers. Cruz sat on the edge of his bed and started taking off his shoes. He stopped to yawn. His brain and body were exhausted.

"Light," Cruz heard Sailor whisper.

Cruz started to request the cabin's environmental computer to increase the light level in the room when Sailor said, louder, "Did you expose the journal to light?"

"Yep," clipped Emmett. He did not turn from his screens. "LED, incandescent, fluorescent, bioluminescent—"

"Sunlight?"

"Naturally."

"How much and for how long?"

He moaned. "I don't know, Sailor. Does it matter?"

"Yes. *Yes!*" She started toward him. "You said the journal is made from plants—bamboo, right?"

Emmett tossed her a look over his shoulder. "And sunflowers."

"Okay. Green plants contain chlorophyll, which allows them to convert sunlight into energy, right? If you expose the journal to sunlight, isn't there a chance that it might activate the plant-based fibers to produce a—"

"Photosynthetic response." Emmett whirled in his chair, his glasses beginning to give off a golden glow. "You may be onto something, Sailor. Cell regeneration in a bio holo-matrix *is* possible. Theoretically. Studies have found that under the right conditions photosynthesis can repair, even restore, a damaged or defective segment of a holo-sequence."

Cruz pointed a shoe at him. "Are you saying—?"

"The journal may be able to repair itself." Emmett gave them a wide smile. "The journal doesn't need us. It never did."

"So, all I have to do is go up on deck, hold the journal up to the sky, and that will fix it?" asked Cruz.

"No." Emmett's grin faded. "The amount of chlorophyll in the paper is so small you'd be standing there for days or weeks."

"Plus, cloudy weather would slow the process," added Sailor. "We need to find a more concentrated light source."

"The CAVE?" suggested Cruz.

"Maybe, but artificial light contains a narrower range of color than natural sunlight. Not enough blue and red." Emmett stroked his chin. "What we need is full-spectrum light. And a lot of it."

"Don't forget water," said Cruz. "Plants need water for photosynthesis."

"And carbon," added Sailor.

"The journal should be able to use its own carbon molecules," said Emmett, "but it would need to pull water from the environment."

"We could mist it," said Cruz, pretending to spray a water bottle.

"That could work. I guess we could program it all into the CAVE and give it a try—"

"I've got it!" shrieked Sailor. "I know where we can get plenty of light *and* water. Come on!" She raced for the door.

"Wait!" called Emmett. "It's twenty minutes to lights-out. We can't just . . . Sailor, at least, tell us where you're going."

Too late. She had already disappeared around the corner.

Emmett looked at Cruz, who could only give his friend a shrug and take off after her. Cruz was wearing one shoe. The other was still in his hand, but he wasn't about to miss this.

Sailor had a good head start. Twenty feet ahead of them, she was rushing down the passage toward the atrium. At the end of the corridor, she sped right and flew up the grand staircase. Cruz followed her up two more flights. He tried to catch her but never closed the gap.

When he hit the top of the stairs at the bridge deck, he saw the end of her ponytail swing out. She was heading to the observation deck. Cruz caught up to her just inside the room, where she had pulled up. The place was empty, thank goodness.

Catching her breath, Sailor could only point at . . .

Chef Kristos's garden!

Cruz's gaze traveled over the greenhouse that took up one end, almost a full quarter of the large compartment. Blinking against the bright lights, he whistled softly. "Solar-powered laser lights."

"And automatic spray misters," said Sailor. "It's everything we need in one spot."

Emmett was 15 seconds behind them. "Perfect . . . don't just stand there . . . running out of time, people," he huffed, rushing past them to the greenhouse door. Cruz and Sailor hurried after him.

Once inside the glass enclosure, they were almost immediately swallowed by an edible jungle. Hanging baskets overflowing with strawberries, peas, eggplants, and various flowers brushed their heads, while broccoli, lettuce, and red peppers sprang up from the waist-high rows of table planters. Around the perimeter, beans, tomatoes, cucumbers, and other vines clung to stakes and trellises, coiling their way up the metal-framed windows. The air was hot and damp and Cruz had to take a few extra breaths to fill his lungs. He glanced up into the circle of bright lights and misters. "We should probably go to the center to get the most light, right?"

"Uh-huh." Emmett was fighting off a nasturtium vine clinging to his comm pin.

In the middle of the garden, Sailor slid a couple of the plant trays apart. "Here's a spot in the herbs." One planter was filled with the soft spikes of rosemary, while the other held long, thin stalks of blooming lavender. "It's got good light, and it's not directly under a mister. We don't want to soak the journal."

Taking his mother's journal from his pocket, Cruz slipped the three-inch-by-three-inch square out of Lani's protective sleeve. He set it flat

on the table between the two trays. They all knew that touch activated the origami sequence. Cruz placed his fingertips on top of the journal.

Three pairs of eyes stared at the wisp of paper. There was nothing to do now but wait.

Sailor ran a hand through the rosemary, sending the piney scent swirling around them. "Well, at least if nothing happens, the journal will smell good," she said.

Cruz grinned. He knew she was trying to ease the tension. On the other side of him, Emmett's glasses had fogged over. Cruz couldn't help but chuckle.

Sailor had seen him and was giggling, too.

Everyone went back to staring at the journal. It was so quiet. So still. So warm.

Another five minutes passed.

Cruz felt beads of sweat collecting on his forehead.

Sailor put up a hand to stifle a yawn.

Emmett wiped off his glasses. "Five minutes to lights-out."

"You guys better go back down," said Cruz. "Who knows how long this could take?"

"You can't stand here all night," said Sailor.

"I don't plan to." Cruz plunked himself down on the floor, crossed his legs, and slid the journal from the table onto his lap. "See? I'll lie down when I get tired. Go on, you guys. There's no sense in all three of us getting into trouble if Taryn finds out we broke curfew. It's okay. Really."

A look passed between Emmett and Sailor.

"Go!" Cruz shooed them away. "I'll be fine."

"Okay, but call us if something happens," said Sailor, hesitantly moving away.

"Or if you need *anything*," added Emmett.

"I will."

An hour later, Cruz was still staring at the unresponsive journal, now balancing on his left knee. He'd taken off his jacket to use as a pillow, but he wasn't sleepy. What he was, was warm. And thirsty.

The mini fridge in the observation area was usually stocked with beverages. Cruz could jet out, grab some water, and be back in two minutes. Five, if he wanted to cool off. Cruz got up. His right foot tingled with numbness. Sliding a corner of the journal under the tray of lavender so it didn't float away, Cruz made his way to the greenhouse entrance. Keeping the branches of a fig tree between himself and the glass, he peered into the observation area. He saw no one. Cruz cracked the door. A blast of cool air swept over his feverish cheeks.

Ahhhhh. That felt good.

Cruz made a beeline to the little fridge at the far corner of the compartment. Three glasses of ice water later he was starting to feel less like a shriveled orange. It was a quarter to 11. Cruz had never before been up on the observation deck so late. Bedtime for the explorers was 9:30 p.m. on weeknights.

Sipping water, Cruz turned to look out the back window. The full, apricot-colored moon made the churning water of the Alboran Sea sparkle like thousands of tiny diamonds. Earlier that day, the ship had passed through the Strait of Gibraltar. They were now off the southern coast of Spain, two days out of Barcelona. The trail of glistening water was beautiful. Peaceful. Steady. It reminded Cruz of home, of lazy days when all that was ahead of him was an afternoon of surfing. He missed Hanalei. And his dad. So much. In the quiet compartment, the what-ifs began piling up in his brain. What if Nebula found out his dad was leaving clues behind? What if Cruz gave Nebula the cipher and they didn't stick to their end of the deal? What if the greenhouse lights didn't fix the journal? What if...?

A thin white trail zipped across the sky. The Leonids!

He had almost forgotten about the meteor shower. Cruz knew that to succeed he needed to focus on the task at hand and push the what-ifs away, but it wasn't easy. It never was. Watching for meteors and talking to himself, Cruz almost didn't hear the voices in the passage. He darted for the greenhouse, barely making it inside before the visitors entered the observation deck. Cruz gently shut the door, then crouched behind a potted fig tree. Cruz wanted to get to the safety of the center of the thick garden, but it was too risky. Any movement might draw attention his way. He'd have to hunker down and wait for them to leave. Whoever it was would probably not stay long anyway. It was likely a couple of crew members on a break.

The greenhouse door was inching open. Someone was coming inside!

Cruz made himself as small as he could. The best he could hope for now was that they wouldn't turn him in to Taryn. Ducking his head, he held his breath.

A snort. "Is that your impression of a fig?"

Peering between the leaves of the tree, Cruz saw Sailor. He exhaled. That was close! Sailor was juggling aluminum water bottles and a handful of granola bars. Emmett was next to her, his arms around several pillows.

Cruz straightened. "What are you guys doing back here?"

Sailor pointed her toe to show she was wearing her pink flamingo slippers. "We're staying with you."

"If Taryn finds out—"

"Then we'll all get in trouble together," said Sailor matter-of-factly. A pair of fluffy flamingos shuffled past him.

"Taryn won't find out." Emmett lifted his wrist. "According to our OS bands, right now we're all in REM sleep and happily dreaming away."

Cruz looked down at his wrist. His OS screen read SLEEP MODE. His jaw fell. "Emmett, how did you—"

A pillow hit him in the chest. "Don't ask."

12

►WITH A NOD to Scorpion and Komodo,
Thorne Prescott stepped inside the rusty silo. The door slammed
behind him with a bone-chilling clang. There was a chair in the
center of the empty round storage building, but Marco Coronado
was not in it. He was seated on the cracked cement on the opposite side of the structure, propped up against the peeling metal of
a curved wall. Legs out. Ankles crossed. Hands folded.

Prescott held up a white take-out bag. "Hope you like Chinese."

Marco didn't answer. Didn't move. Panic swept through
Prescott. Scorpion and Komodo . . . had they . . . ?

Was Marco . . . ?

Prescott charged forward.

"Fine," rasped Marco.

Prescott took a deep breath and let his heartbeat return to
normal. He set the bag next to Marco, along with a cup of coffee,
then backed up several feet so he was not close enough to be
taken by surprise. "You'd better eat. We'll be leaving soon."

"Is Cruz all right?"

"As far as I know."

"Somehow, that doesn't ease my mind."

Prescott didn't expect it would.

"Do you really have a son?" asked Marco. "Or was that for my
benefit?"

Prescott had told Marco the lie back at the Goofy Foot to gain
his trust. He considered lying again, but something compelled
him to honesty. "No children. A niece."

"What you're doing . . . it can't just be for the money," said

Marco. "You don't seem that lazy. Or cruel."

"People aren't always what they seem."

After a moment, Marco reached for the bag.

The door opened behind Prescott. Scorpion leaned in.

"Cobra, we're just waiting on the go from the boys at Gemini. Oh, and Komodo's altitude meds. The last thing we need is a three-hundred-pound guy hurling out the window the whole way up Mauna K—"

"Do what you have to do," hissed Prescott. "But make it quick."

"Excuse me." Marco was holding up a chopstick. "Can I get a knife and fork?"

"No," growled Scorpion.

"Yes," countered Prescott, and when his partner looked at him in disbelief, he clarified. "A butter knife. You can manage that, I think."

The door swung shut.

Marco dipped the chopsticks into the white box. "You won't get what you're after."

Prescott folded his arms and stared up at the funnel-shaped metal roof. "I think we will. If your son wants to see you alive again, he'll give us the cipher pieces."

"I'm sure Cruz will do exactly as you instruct. Not that it will matter."

"What do you mean by that?"

"Only that no one can change the past." Marco held up his chopsticks, suspiciously inspecting the fried dumpling between them. "Not even Nebula."

13

▶ **CRUZ FLUTTERED** his eyelids.

He was lying on his side on the floor of the greenhouse, his right arm crushed under him. It hurt. His lower back was aching, too, thanks to the ceramic tile bed.

"Hi, Cruzer."

"Mom!" He popped upright, smacking his forehead on a corner of the plant table. Cruz's gaze went from the pointed orb on the floor to the holographic image of his mother it projected above him and back to the ball again.

It had worked! While they'd slept, the device had managed to fix whatever was malfunctioning. Cruz's touch had triggered the identification protocol, which had confirmed his identity and opened the journal. Cruz wondered how long his mom had been standing—hovering—there. He hoped not too long, even though she was only a hologram and, technically, had all the time in the world.

Rubbing his head, Cruz looked up at her. "You have no idea how good it is to see you."

"It's good to see you, too," she said. Cruz knew it was a preprogrammed response, yet it still sent a warmth through him.

Cruz leaned in to shake his sleeping roommate's shoulder. "Emmett?"

Rolling away from him, his friend let out a grunt.

Cruz reached to his other side. Sailor was on her back. "Sailor!"

"I'm up, I'm up," she croaked, flinging a hand over her eyes. "What time is it?"

"Um . . . a quarter to five."

"Too. Early. Must. Sleep."

"Cruz, do you have the second piece of the cipher?" asked his mom, sliding a lock of long blond hair over one shoulder.

At that, Emmett bolted upright. He fumbled for his glasses. "She's here . . . Your mom's here . . . It worked. I can't believe it actually worked!"

Sailor was slowly raising herself up onto her elbows. When she saw the image floating next to her, she gasped. "Wow! We did it! I mean *it* did it—"

"*You* did it," corrected Cruz. He put up a palm, and she slapped it.

"Cruz, do you have the second piece of the cipher?" repeated his mother. They knew she could not give him the third clue until she had confirmed that the second stone was genuine.

Cruz's hand automatically went to his neck. "I . . . I do, Mom, but I don't have it here."

"What?" squealed Sailor. "What do you mean, you don't have it here? Where is it?" When Cruz didn't answer right away, she leaned in to glare at Emmett, who lifted a shoulder. "He wouldn't tell me."

"I didn't want to take it with me to the Halloween party," explained Cruz. "And once I discovered that Nebula knew I wore it, I figured it wasn't safe on the lanyard either. So I . . . I hid it. I . . . I didn't tell you guys. I figured you'd be in danger if you knew. And I didn't bring it last night because you rushed up here so fast . . ."

"Okay, okay." Sailor waved. "Go get it now."

"It's . . . uh . . . not that easy."

"We should probably wait anyway," said Emmett, reaching for his tablet. "Everyone's going to be up soon. I bet Chef Kristos and the breakfast crew are already in the galley. For all we know, somebody could be headed up here right now to get fresh fruits and veggies for breakfast."

Cruz nodded. "Plus, Lani would kill me if we unlocked the next clue without her."

"I understand," said his mother. "Initiating shutdown."

"NO!" shouted Cruz, Emmett, and Sailor at once.

"Wait, Mom, wait! Do not shut down. *Do not shut down.*" Cruz hopped to his feet, holding his hands out toward her. "Emmett!" he called over his shoulder. "Can we be sure that if we close the journal, we'll be able to open it again?"

Emmett was madly typing on his tablet. "I'm syncing with the interface now. I'll try to access the diagnostics to see exactly what the problem was and how it was repaired, so that if it happens again, we'll know what to do. Also, I'm uploading a program I wrote that will allow backdoor access in case this happens again . . . Uh-huh . . . uh-huh . . ."

"What is it?" pressed Sailor, scurrying to peer over his shoulder.

"Hold on . . . Uh-huh . . . uh-huh . . ."

"Emmett!" cried Cruz.

"One second," said Sailor. "He's almost there."

"Uh-huh . . . Aha! According to the diagnostic, it was a damaged circuit in the origami robotic progression. See, it's programmed not to begin the morphing process if it can't finish it. Once a link in the chain was broken, the activator simply shut off. That's why whatever we tried had no effect. There was nothing we could have done."

"Are we good?" asked Cruz.

"Not yet... not yet..."

"Emmett!"

Finally, his roommate's head came up. "Upload is complete."

"You can shut down," Cruz instructed his mother. He lifted a hand to her fading image. "See you in a little while, Mom."

She smiled.

Cruz's breath caught. He had not expected that. It's what was so strange about this whole experience. Cruz was used to holograms, holo-videos, and time capsules—devices that could capture a memory for you to relive as often as you wanted. But the journal was different. It held surprises. Cruz was never sure what his mother would say or do next. It was like...

Life.

Grabbing their pillows and water bottles, the trio hurried down to the explorers' deck.

"Let's meet tonight at nine in our cabin," Cruz whispered to Sailor as they dropped her off at her stateroom. "I'll text Lani." He knew this was one text she would not ignore.

Cruz already had a plan to retrieve the cipher stones before classes began that morning. He'd shower, dress, eat breakfast, and arrive at Taryn's cabin with a good half hour to spare before conservation class. He would offer to walk Hubbard, which his adviser would happily let him do because she would be dealing with at least one explorer who had lost something, broken something, needed something, or was sick with something. Cruz would take Hubbard to his personal meadow, swiftly retrieve the cipher from the pocket of the life vest, and return the Westie to his owner. It would be a snap!

Except it wasn't. A snap.

When Cruz knocked on Taryn's door, she didn't answer. She was usually an early riser, and he hadn't seen her at breakfast. She must already be walking Hubbard. Cruz trotted down to the end of the explorers' passage and through the door to the aft sundeck. No Taryn. No Hubbard.

He retraced his steps. Sometimes Taryn left her stateroom unlocked. Maybe this was one of those times. Maybe Hubbard was inside. Cruz put his hand on the doorknob. It would take him less than 30 seconds to slip in, get the stones, and slip out again. He slowly turned the knob...

"She's not there."

Cruz jumped.

"Sorry," said Bryndis, breathing hard. She was in shorts, a tee, and sneakers—had just come back from her jog, obviously. "Didn't mean to scare you."

"You didn't," he lied.

"I knocked a few minutes ago during my cooldown. She's probably at breakfast."

Cruz shook his head. "I just came from there."

"Is it important?" Bryndis tapped the spot on her collarbone where the explorers wore their comm pins to signal he could call Taryn.

"Not a big deal," said Cruz. "I'll find her at lunch."

But at lunchtime, Taryn was a no-show in the dining room. She wasn't in her cabin either. This time, Cruz was able to try the door uninterrupted. It was locked. After classes were over for the day, he stopped by Taryn's cabin again. Still no answer. Cruz was beginning to worry. It wasn't like Taryn to disappear like this.

There was only one thing left to do. Standing in the middle of the explorers' passage, he tapped his comm pin. "Cruz Coronado to Taryn Secliff."

A few seconds later: "Taryn here."

That was a relief!

"I came by your cabin to...uh..." Cruz was so glad she was all right that his mind went blank. "...to play with Hubbard."

"He can't play right now."

Her voice sounded strange. Chilly. Distant. Their explorer-sitter, as Dugan jokingly referred to her, was a no-nonsense person, but she was not unfriendly. And she was certainly never dismissive, not when it came to her explorers.

"Taryn, is everything okay?" asked Cruz.

"I'm sorry … it's just …" She cleared her throat. "Do you have time to come up here?"

He had 40 minutes before he was due in the library to meet the rest of his team to finish their looting assignment. "Yes. Where are you?"

"Sick bay."

Sick bay? Something *was* wrong!

Hubbard!

"I'll be right there." His heart thumping against his ribs, Cruz dashed down the explorers' passage. He charged up two flights of stairs and down the fourth-deck passage, not slowing until he reached the last compartment. Cruz slid to a stop inside sick bay, nearly colliding with Taryn, who was standing in the small reception area. "Hubbard … what's the matter? Is he hurt or sick, which one?" cried Cruz, a cramp slicing into his side.

Taryn quickly shook her head.

Oh no! No! He was too late!

Digging his fingers into the sides of his waist, Cruz fell forward. A wave of sadness overwhelmed him. Tears sprang to his eyes. What could have happened? And how? Hubbard was perfectly fine yesterday. "Oh, Taryn," choked Cruz, feeling himself crumple. "I loved him. I loved him so much."

A hand was on his back. "Cruz? Hubbard's okay."

His head shot up.

"He's here for his annual exam with Dr. Eikenboom," said Taryn.

"Then he's not …?"

"He's a healthy two-year-old pup with more energy than all of you explorers combined."

Cruz let out the longest sigh of his life. "It's just that … I've been trying to find you all day, and when I finally did you asked me to come up here … and you sounded funny, I thought … I thought …"

"The worst." She sucked in her lower lip. "Sorry about that. I've been going nonstop since I rolled out of bed this morning. First, I had to deal with Kat and Yulia's exploding showerhead, and shortly after that, an exploding chef. Chef Kristos is insistent someone is stealing from his herb garden."

"Oh yeah?" squeaked Cruz, thinking of the herb trays they had moved. That's when it hit him. *The cipher!* In all the excitement, he had forgotten that Hubbard still carried the stone pieces in his life vest. At least, Cruz hoped he did. The doctor or Taryn most certainly would have removed the vest for the dog's exam. It's possible one of them had discovered the cipher hidden inside!

Taryn was still talking. "After that, I had to send back a shipment of hats and gloves, which were, unfortunately, made for giants, not explorers. And since we're putting in at Port Vell in Barcelona tomorrow, I spent most of the afternoon confirming our transportation, dining, and . . . other activities." She puckered her lips. "Oh, and then I had to track down a retainer that went MIA—"

"Tao lost it again?"

"No one will be happier than I when that girl's teeth are straight." She shook a finger at him. "And you did *not* hear me say that. Anyway, after that crisis, I had Hubbard's exam, which brings me to why I asked you up here. I need a favor. Dr. Eikenboom is giving Hubbard his shots, so it shouldn't be long, but I'm supposed to be in a conference call with Dr. Hightower in exactly four minutes, and you know how she doesn't like to be kept waiting—"

"And you want me to bring Hubbard back down?"

"Would you?"

"Sure," said Cruz. "We'll make a pit stop at his meadow, too."

"Thanks, you're a lifesaver."

"Um . . . what about his life vest?"

"That's right, the nurse has it—could you get that, too?"

Cruz nodded. He'd be able to check to see if the cipher was still in the side pocket.

"And I haven't forgotten about you." She reached for her tablet. "You're on my to-do list."

"Me? What did I do wrong?"

"You can pretend everything's okay, Cruz Coronado, but I know you're worried about your dad and your aunt, too."

"Taryn, I'm fine, really—"

"I'll be the judge of that." She looked at the clock. "We *will* talk later." It wasn't a request.

Catching the doorjamb on her way out, Taryn tapped it. "Oh, and, Cruz?"

He turned, expecting more instructions.

"Hubbard loves you, too."

WITH FELIPE'S VIOLIN serenading them through the walls, Cruz dimmed the lights in the cabin. Everyone had agreed to meet in cabin 202 early tonight, to adjust for the 12-hour time difference between the Mediterranean and Hawaii. While the day was winding down for Cruz and his friends, it was just beginning for Lani. Cruz knelt at the little round table between the pair of navy chairs. "Here we go. Ready?"

"Ready," said Sailor. She had settled into one of the chairs, her legs tucked under her and her tablet on her lap.

Emmett was in the other chair, also with his tablet, but he was hugging the penguin pillow so tightly its poor beak was bent. "Me too," he said.

From her bedroom in Hanalei, Lani was twisting her hair. The second she'd answered his call, Cruz had blurted, "Promise that you won't go to the abandoned sugar mill."

"But the clue—"

"Promise. It's too dangerous."

Lani had given him her sour-lemon face. "Fine."

Cruz slid the journal from its protective cover by the edges and set it on the table. He tapped it with his index finger, then drew back. Like him, Sailor was frozen. Lani, too. Emmett's mouth was moving. No sound was coming out, but Cruz could lip-read the word: "Please."

He joined in the silent chant. *Please. Please. Please.*

At first, nothing. A few more seconds passed. And then—something. The page twitched.

A flap appeared. It unfolded from the center of the square. The first flap was followed by another, then another. Faster and faster the flaps appeared, creased, and folded. They went quickly, going this way and that, up and down, corner to corner, building layer upon layer until they had created a ball covered with dozens of small triangles.

"Yes!" shouted Lani once the journal had completed its transformation into a multi-pointed orb.

Cruz, however, said nothing. He knew they weren't out of the woods yet.

Seconds later, an orange light appeared at one of the tips that faced Sailor. She quickly spun the ball to direct the light at Cruz. The beam steadily swept over his face, chest, and stomach. It shut off. This was the real test. Would the journal open a second time?

Nobody moved. Cruz felt almost as warm as he had in the greenhouse. "Hi, Cruzer."

Cruz exhaled. Emmett fell back into his chair. Sailor and Lani clapped.

"Hi, Mom," laughed Cruz.

"Cruz, do you have the second piece of the cipher?" She flipped her long blond hair over one shoulder the same way she had the first time she'd asked him that question.

Extending his arm, Cruz uncurled his fingers to show her the stone in his palm. He'd had no trouble getting it. Both pieces of the cipher had been right where Cruz had left them, safe and sound inside the tiny pocket of Hubbard's yellow life vest. The Westie had been a good watchdog, even if he hadn't realized it.

"Well done," said his mother. "This is a genuine piece. You have unlocked a new clue."

The explorers cheered but quickly quieted down as Petra Coronado continued speaking.

"To find the third cipher, travel to the ancient rose city of stone. Walk on confetti until you find the animal that is at home both in the clouds and under the sea. It may seem like a strange mythical creature, but at the end of the day, if you're willing to reach out, you'll have your reward."

Cruz frowned. The rose city? That seemed awfully general. There were probably lots of cities with that nickname.

"You'll figure it out," said his mother, seeming to read his mind. "Unfortunately, I have no one I can send you to if you need help. This time, Cruzer, I'm afraid you're on your own."

"I'll be okay, Mom." He tried to sound brave, but inside he was shriveling.

As they got to work on the clue, Cruz tried not to show that he was upset. But he was. And about so many things. The most important, of course, was his father. Each minute that ticked by was one more minute his dad was in the hands of the enemy. It was almost more than he could bear, which is why Cruz had to turn his mind to something else whenever he did think about it. He was also worried about Aunt Marisol and Lani. If one or both of them got too close to the truth, there was no telling what Nebula would do. And then there was Jericho Miles. Cruz had no idea what to make of him. Why was he on board *Orion*? What was the Synthesis doing behind the secret door two decks down? Were they here for the advancement of science or for him? Finally, there was the cipher. Making a decoy had seemed like a good idea when Sailor had suggested it, but now Cruz wasn't so sure. What if Nebula caught on? Despite Cruz's best efforts to keep his plans secret, Nebula always seemed to find out what he was up to. With his father's life on the line, it didn't seem smart to try to fool them.

All these problems—how did he begin to sort them out? If only Cruz could talk things through with his dad or Aunt Marisol the way he was used to doing. But, of course, that was impossible.

Sailor was frowning at him. "You don't like the idea?"

"Sorry. What idea?"

"We thought we'd search for the rose city, you know, start with a location."

"That...that sounds fine," he said.

"Let's make a list of everything we can find that mentions it," said Emmett, reaching for his tablet. "Tomorrow, we'll start sorting through it all and narrow things down."

Cruz nodded his approval, but his head was swimming. In the end, all his doubts and worries and fears amounted to one thought—a question, really. It was one terrifying what-if that he could not ignore.

What if Cruz couldn't save his dad?

BARCELONA,
SPAIN

Bay of Biscay

FRANCE

ANDORRA

PORTUGAL

SPAIN

Balearic Sea

Mediterranean Sea

MOROCCO

ALGERIA

CRUZ SQUISHED his nose against the

window. He was riding in the second of two vans carrying the explorers
from the harbor into downtown Barcelona.

Squinting up into the mid-morning sun, Cruz tried to catch a glimpse
of an iron statue perched atop a 200-foot pillar. Unfortunately, all he
could see was an arm pointing out to the western Mediterranean. Lining
the opposite side of the four-lane ring of pavement were several grand
buildings. Their Roman columns and pointed rooflines reminded Cruz of
the Academy's headquarters in Washington, D.C. The only difference that
he could see in the quick moment was that above each of these structures, the red-and-yellow flag of Spain flapped in the November wind.
They sailed past a pale yellow castle-like building with arched windows
and scrollwork balconies. In the seat in front of him, Bryndis pointed to
the winged-lion statues proudly standing guard on the roof. "It looks like
something right out of a fairy tale."

The next block down, a glint of sunlight off metal blinded Cruz. Blinking away the spots, he saw a series of thin silver hoops rising from the
brick sidewalk. They were so tall they easily curled over the palm trees
and so wide that a couple of the rings straddled the intersection.

"It's called Onades," said Emmett, who was next to Bryndis. He was
wearing his GPS sunglasses over his regular emoto-glasses. Fanchon's
GPS, which could be activated by either the explorers' sunglasses or the

Earth pins on their lapels, projected opaque images of street maps, monuments, tourist attractions, and other points of interest for any city in the world. "It's made up of seven stainless-steel arches, is one hundred thirty-eight feet high, and weighs more than three thousand pounds," said Emmett, reading the text in his sunglasses. "It was designed by artist Andreu Alfaro. Constructed in 2003, it is meant to represent the waves crashing onto Barcelona's coast."

As they drove through the bustling city, Cruz saw modern shops, hotels, and outdoor cafés nestled between Gothic churches and buildings. None of the explorers knew where they were going. Professor Luben had come with them, as had Monsieur Legrand and Taryn. Cruz suspected another competition was in their future. Monsieur Legrand was here to see that they had a good workout while Taryn had come along to make sure it was fun. How Professor Luben fit into the mix, however, was a mystery. He was sitting a few rows in front of Cruz and Emmett and recounting another one of his adventures for the explorers around him. This one was about cave diving at a Florida sinkhole called Eagle's Nest. "You dive down through this tube that's maybe six feet wide, and at a depth of seventy feet, it opens up into a cave that's so big and so dark you can't see a thing." Professor Luben put his hands in front of his face. "It's blackness, pure blackness. The cave is so big they call it the Ballroom. So many divers have died in Eagle's Nest, there's even a warning sign telling inexperienced divers to go back!"

Cruz had a feeling Professor Luben would love to hear the details of the quest for Cruz's mom's formula, but of course, that was impossible. He knew he could share nothing beyond his circle of friends—not even the small victories, like the one last night.

In the short time they'd had before it was time for bed, Cruz, Emmett, Lani, and Sailor had knuckled down to try to answer the first part of his mom's clue: Where was the rose city? At Emmett's suggestion, they had taken out their tablets and started searching.

"There are a bunch of cities with the name Rose in them," Lani had pointed out. "Most are in America, but there are a couple in Italy…one in France…a Rose Valley in Pakistan."

"Portland, Oregon, is nicknamed the Rose City," said Sailor.

"There's a holo-game called *City of the White Rose*," offered Emmett.

Cruz had stopped typing to stare at his search results. Could it be that simple?

The lights flickered.

"Ugh!" said Sailor. "Two minutes to lights-out."

"That went too fast," said Lani.

"I…uh…think we can stop brainstorming," said Cruz.

"Like we have a choice," sighed Emmett.

"That's not what I meant," said Cruz, and he began to read the article on his tablet. "More than two thousand years ago, a nomadic Arab tribe called the Nabataeans settled in the mountains of southern Jordan. They created a luxurious regional trading center, carving elaborate temples, tombs, churches, and even an amphitheater from the red sandstone cliffs. The Nabataeans called their rose-colored city of stone"—Cruz glanced up—"Petra."

Nobody moved. Everyone knew Petra was his mom's first name.

"That has to be it, Cruz," said Lani. "Petra has to be where she hid the third piece of the cipher!"

They had all agreed.

Cruz had been too excited to sleep. He'd stayed awake well past midnight, looking at photos of the Rose City on his tablet. Petra was spread out over 100 square miles and at its peak had been home to more than 20,000 people! The cipher could be anywhere—hidden within Al-Khazneh, an intricate 128-foot-tall royal tomb, or tucked between one of the rows of the Nabataean Theater, a massive amphitheater carved into the rock face. Or it could be in any one of Petra's hundreds of ancient temples, monuments, or tombs. Cruz kept repeating the second part of his mom's clue until he had it memorized. Only then did he drift off into a fitful sleep.

> *Walk on confetti until you find the animal that is at home both in the clouds and under the sea. It may seem like a strange mythical creature, but at the end of the day, if you're willing to reach out, you'll have your reward.*

Cruz's van was pulling into a circular driveway. The two vehicles parked next to a tall, curved, peach-colored sandstone wall. Red ivy curled up from the bottom of the wall, reaching to a row of notches cut into the top, like on every castle in every movie Cruz had ever seen. Stepping out of the van into the sunshine, Cruz caught a glimpse of a round castle tower behind a massive iron gate.

Taryn motioned for them to gather around her. "Welcome to Desvalls Palace. It dates back to 1791 and was constructed by Joan Antoni Desvalls i d'Ardena, marquis of Llupia and Alfarrás. It is home to the oldest garden in Barcelona. Now it's a public park. The castle is used as a library and gardening institute, but we won't be going inside." She gave them a wicked grin. "Today, we have other plans for you. Come with me." Taryn led the way around the outside of the wall to a wooded walkway. The wide, tree-lined brick-and-cement path wound behind the palace.

They strolled past terraced gardens, manicured hedges, Greek statues, and gates that led to more terraced gardens and manicured hedges and Greek statues. The place was huge!

"You ready?" Emmett hissed to Cruz as they walked.

"For what?"

"We must be doing something for anthro class. Why else would Professor Luben have come with us? And if it *is* an anthro assignment, they'll be giving us PANDA units."

Cruz saw what his roommate was getting at. He needed a PANDA to make the decoy cipher. It would take only a few minutes to make a quick scan of the two cipher pieces now in the front pocket of his uniform jacket and upload the results to his tablet. They could then make the fakes on the 3D printer in their cabin.

"I'm ready," said Cruz. He didn't want to say anything to Emmett here, but he was still concerned about giving Nebula the decoy. It was an awfully big risk—one that he wasn't sure he wanted to take. He was considering another idea. What if Cruz made a duplicate of the cipher for himself and gave Nebula the real thing? It would mean that Nebula had an accurate cipher, of course, but his father would be out of danger.

Taryn was taking them down a long path with cypress trees on one side. The 20-foot-tall evergreen trees were packed tightly together, pruned into one long, neat rectangular hedge. Cruz wondered what was on the other side, but the branches were so dense he couldn't peek through them. It was probably another garden. They passed a cypress archway but didn't go under it. It wasn't until they went up a series of stone steps onto a landing with a pair of stone gazebos and turned to face back where they'd come from did things become clear. The hedge was the outer perimeter of many, many other hedges. This was a giant maze!

"You're looking at Parc del Laberint d'Horta, the Labyrinth Park of Horta," announced Taryn. She moved to the carved sandstone railing. It overlooked the square maze that was a bit smaller than a football field.

"From up here, it looks easy, doesn't it?" Taryn grinned. "Don't be fooled. This maze contains more than two thousand twists and turns. Also, we're throwing in a few twists of our own, which Monsieur Legrand will explain in a moment. If you do make it to the center of the labyrinth, however, you'll be greeted by a statue of Eros, the Greek god of love, as well as Professor Luben, who is also lovely but not a god, I'm afraid."

Everyone laughed.

"*Attention, s'il vous plaît!*" bellowed Monsieur Legrand. "Each team will consist of two quiz contestants, two spotters, and two runners. Team Cousteau, because you're down a member, you'll have one spotter, which actually might be the better deal when you see what we've got planned. Here's how it will work: Each team gets one try at the maze, while the other teams wait out of sight. Taryn will be our quizmaster. She'll ask your two contestants a question about Spain, and if you've done all of your assigned readings, it should not be difficult. The contestants will have a minute to confer and give an answer. If the answer is correct, the two runners will get thirty seconds to move through the maze, then must stop. They'll get an additional thirty seconds for every correct answer. The runners will get navigational help from their spotters, who will tell them whether to turn right or left, move forward or back, and so on. The spotters will be up here at the rail with their GPS sunglasses linked to a drone flying overhead. The drone cam will give the spotters a complete view of the labyrinth. The spotters will also be wearing headsets to help their runners navigate the maze. Runners will be able to hear the contestants and the spotters; however, they will not be able to talk to them. If the contestants *don't* answer correctly, fifteen seconds will be added to your overall time and Taryn will move on to the next question.

The goal, of course, is to get through the maze as quickly as possible. I will be the timekeeper. Once both runners touch the statue in the center of the labyrinth, Professor Luben will tell me to stop the clock. The team with the best time will win a special honor, which Professor Luben will reveal at the end of the game. Everyone clear on the rules?" When they nodded, Monsieur Legrand rolled up the sleeves of his black turtleneck. "Oh, there's one more thing."

"Wuh-oh," Emmett muttered to Cruz, "here it comes."

"The two runners will be tethered together."

The explorers groaned.

"Teams will not be allowed to watch other teams do the maze, even once they have finished," said Taryn. "Nor will you know the time of your team or any team until the competition is complete. You will go in alphabetical order: Cousteau, Earhart, Galileo, and Magellan. Please get into your teams now. Professor Luben, Monsieur Legrand, and I will come around to designate who will be contestants, spotters, and runners."

"You mean we don't get to choose?" asked Dugan. When Taryn shook her head, he puffed up his cheeks; however, he didn't complain.

Cruz knew how Dugan felt. He wished they could have chosen, too. He wanted to be a runner. That sounded fun!

Professor Luben was coming toward them, carrying a small black velvet bag. "Team Cousteau, in this pouch are five holo-chips with your images on them. I will pick the first quiz contestant." Wiggling his fingers like a magician about to pull a rabbit out of his hat, he stuck his hand into the bag. He took out a flat, round poker chip, looked at it, then held it up. A 3D image of Sailor's head stared at them. Professor Luben turned to Sailor. "Your turn. You'll pick the second contestant."

Digging into the bag, Sailor brought out Emmett's chip.

Yes! Cruz cheered silently. Emmett and Sailor were going to answer the questions for their team. They would do well.

"Now, for your two runners. Choose the first one, please." Professor Luben held the bag out to Emmett. He reached in and wasted no time pulling out a chip. They huddled up to see whose face was on it. "It's Cruz," said their teacher.

Yes, again! Two for two.

"Select your partner." Professor Luben held the open bag out to Cruz. "The person on the remaining chip will be your spotter."

Cruz felt his stomach tighten. Only Bryndis and Dugan were left. Cruz did *not* want to be tethered to Dugan Marsh, even for a game that wasn't graded. He had a fifty-fifty shot. Bryndis was standing behind Dugan's shoulder, her hands up to her chin and the first two fingers on each hand tightly crossed. She was grinning at Cruz. She wanted to run with him. Taking a deep breath, Cruz plunged a fist into the velvet pouch. The chips all felt the same. Round. Smooth. Flat. He went back and forth between the two disks. Which one should he choose? Cruz closed his hand around a chip, brought it up, and uncurled his fingers to see...

Dugan.

Cruz tried to keep his disappointment inside, but he had a feeling his forced grin looked more like the face you make when you smack your funny bone.

"Dugan and Cruz, you'll run. Bryndis, you'll be their spotter," said Professor Luben. "You're the first team up, so go get your headsets and prepare. Runners will start at the far south corner of the maze by the arch we passed on the way in. Cruz and Dugan, I'll get the tether and meet you down there to connect you."

Ten minutes later, with the other teams in another part of the park, Team Cousteau was in position. Sailor and Emmett had taken their place in front of Taryn on the stone terrace. Bryndis was a few feet away, facing the maze. She wore a headset and her GPS sunglasses, linked to the drone cam hovering 50 feet above them. Cruz and Dugan had their backs to the entrance, marked by the cypress arch over tall marble carvings of two robed figures—likely a Greek god and goddess, Cruz figured. They had been instructed not to turn around until Monsieur Legrand gave the signal. Cruz watched Professor Luben tie one end of a clear, flexible three-foot band to his left wrist and the other end to Dugan's right wrist. "By the way, I meant to tell you," said their anthropology teacher, "remember the looting tile your team flagged with the underground circles?"

"Yes!" Cruz and Dugan said at the same time. They had been anxiously waiting for news.

"I consulted a few colleagues, and we agree it's an unreported archaeological site."

"What is it?" pressed Dugan.

"We don't know. Yet. Which is why, if I were you, I'd *really* want to win this contest."

Cruz didn't understand. "What do you—"

"Take your marks!" Monsieur Legrand's voice boomed in Cruz's head. He heard Professor Luben's footsteps rush down the dirt path into the maze.

"Here we go!" Taryn came over their headsets. "First question. Emmett and Sailor, the southern and eastern coasts of Spain often experience warm winds that originate in northern Africa. What is the name of these winds?"

A beat later, Emmett burst, "Sirocco! Sorry, Sailor."

"It's okay," she chuckled.

"Correct," said Taryn.

Dugan and Cruz looked sideways at each other. Any second now Monsieur Legrand was going to say—

"Go, Team Cousteau!"

Cruz whirled right. Dugan went left. The flexible tube between them stretched to its full length, then snapped back, yanking them together. The boys cracked elbows. Dugan stumbled forward. Cruz caught him and set him upright, before spinning them both around to face the entrance. "We've got to work together!" shouted Cruz.

"No kidding," spit Dugan. "I think you broke my arm."

"We're wasting time. Which way should we go? Left or right?"

Dugan pointed to the left. "I want to go that way."

In his head, Cruz heard a calm voice say, "Start to the right."

Bryndis!

There wasn't enough room in the passage between the trees for them to run side by side, so since Cruz was to the right of Dugan, he took the lead. Dugan slipped in behind him without an argument. A miracle.

"Run to the end of the hedge, take a quick left, then a sharp right and get into the far-right lane," instructed Bryndis.

Cruz saw the hedge wall straight ahead, but Dugan was pulling him back. He was slowing down to take their first left, which would take them off course. "Does she mean take the left here...?"

"No," called Cruz, yanking his teammate to the end of the row.

"Hey, we're supposed to be a team," barked Dugan.

"Keep running!" called Cruz, as they took the zigzag, then dashed down the row. "And I'm glad to know you actually care about *our* team."

"What's that supposed to mean?"

They had come to a three-way intersection.

"Take the middle one," said Bryndis.

They did. The pair charged down a long passage with no turns, which gave Cruz a chance to finish his thought. "You spend a lot of time hanging out with Team Magellan."

"Ali's my roommate," huffed Dugan.

"*I'm* your teammate."

"Yeah, but you guys don't like me."

"Stop!" ordered Monsieur Legrand.

Dugan and Cruz pulled up. They'd come to a halt next to a section of the maze where new trees had been planted, their young branches tied to a wire trellis. The pair could easily see into the next row over. Not that it helped much. They had no idea if their passage led to that row or somewhere else. Cruz put his hands on his hips to catch his breath. He looked at Dugan, who was scowling. "You've got it backward, Dugan," said Cruz. "It's like you're competing against us, instead of the other teams."

Dugan kicked at the dirt. "I want to win the North Star."

"At the expense of our team? That's pretty selfish."

"Maybe I have to be selfish," spit Dugan. "I'm the only one looking out for me."

Cruz threw up his untethered hand. "I can't talk to you."

"Then don't."

"Don't worry, from now on, I won't!"

"Second question," said Taryn. "In the early twenty-first century, the population of this wild cat native to southwestern Spain numbered less than one hundred, but it was brought back from the brink of extinction thanks to extraordinary efforts by conservationists. Name this species of cat."

Cruz saw a flash of black. Behind Dugan's shoulder, on the other side of the thinning hedge, somebody was hurrying past. Someone else was in the maze. Probably a tourist.

"The Iberian lynx," Cruz heard Sailor say.

The tourist turned Cruz's way. A hood fell. Cruz saw a mass of wiry red hair and a red beard. Their eyes met for an instant. Then he was gone.

Cruz stood dumbfounded. He couldn't believe it. Was that...?

No, it couldn't be. Not here! Not now!

"Come on!" Dugan was yanking on their tether. "What are you waiting for?"

Cruz hadn't heard Taryn confirm that Sailor's answer was right. He hadn't heard the "go" signal from Monsieur Legrand. His mind reeling, Cruz stumbled after Dugan.

Had he imagined it? Or had Cruz actually come within feet of a man who'd tried to kill him, former Academy librarian and Nebula assassin Malcolm Rook?

15

"**RIGHT** . . . no, *vinstri*," cried Bryndis.

"She means left," called Cruz. Whenever Bryndis got excited, she reverted to her native Icelandic. She'd done it twice in the seven legs they had run so far. Fortunately, their communications/translator pins had caught it, so after the first time, Cruz knew what to listen for.

"Oops, I meant left," said Bryndis.

Correcting his course, Cruz stepped on Dugan's foot. "Sorry."

"Sure you are."

"I *am*."

"Stop!" called Monsieur Legrand.

They obeyed.

Wheezing, Cruz put his hands on his hips. "Dugan, we're going to lose if we don't work together. Can we at least agree on that?"

"Yeah," mumbled his partner.

"If we have to go *vinstri*, you take the lead since you're on the left. If we need to go *hægri*, I'll take the lead since I'm on the right."

"Fine," grumbled Dugan.

Two could play at that game. "Fine." Cruz spun away so he wouldn't have to look at Dugan.

No. No! It wasn't fine. None of this was fine, and it had to stop. Now.

Cruz spun back. "I'm sorry you don't think we like you, Dugan, but you haven't given us much of a chance. You complain about stuff, you criticize people, you put down ideas—"

"I tell the truth."

"Can't you think of something *nice* to say once in a while? Just one word? To any of us?"

Dugan opened his mouth.

"Go!" shouted Monsieur Legrand

Cruz and Dugan had been so busy arguing they had missed the question and the answer.

"What are you waiting for?" cried Bryndis. "Run! And take your next left."

They took off. Dugan shot out into the lead with Cruz a split second behind him. They followed the maze as it whipped them left, then right, then left again. They had gone through so many twists and turns, Cruz had no idea which direction they were facing.

"At the next intersection, go right," said Bryndis. Dugan slid to the side to let Cruz go by.

It was a smooth exchange, and when Monsieur Legrand ordered them to stop, Cruz and Dugan both knew that this had been their best leg so far.

"Better," said Dugan.

"Much," agreed Cruz.

"See?"

"See, what?"

Dugan gave a sly smile. "I can think of one nice word."

Cruz let himself return the grin.

"Sailor and Emmett, you haven't missed a single question," said Taryn. "Well done. Here is your ninth question. Where in northern Spain can you find Paleolithic art of animals like bison, horses, and goats, as well as handprints dating back to 35,000 B.C.?"

Cruz knew the answer. It was the Cave of Altamira. He'd hoped they would get to explore it, but Professor Luben had told them it was not open to visitors. So many tourists had visited the cave over the years they had altered the temperature and humidity, damaging some of the art. Now only scientists were allowed inside, and they had to wear protective suits. The best the explorers could do was visit a re-creation of the cave built nearby.

Dugan was tapping him. "Altamira, right?"

"Yep."

"I'm sorry I'm so negative," said Dugan. "I don't mean to be. I have a lot on my mind."

"Like . . . ?"

He heard a sigh. "It's . . . my family . . . Don't tell anybody, but I may have to leave the Academy."

"What?"

"The Cave of Altamira," replied Emmett.

"Correct."

There was no time to talk more. The boys got set.

"Go!" called Monsieur Legrand.

"Straight to the end, then *vinstri,*" said Bryndis. "I mean, left."

Cruz moved over to let Dugan go ahead.

"You're almost there," cried Bryndis. "You're almost to the finish. Take your second right and you'll see the entrance to the center. Second *hægri . . . second* right."

Barreling around the last turn, Dugan and Cruz flew through a cypress arch. They lunged for the statue. Cruz jumped to grab an ankle, while Dugan clung to the round sandstone base.

"Time!" called Professor Luben.

Cruz and Dugan collapsed onto their backs, heaving. They had done it! They had made it through the Horta labyrinth. But had they gone fast enough to win? They'd have to wait and see.

Cruz held up his left forearm, palm out. His chest still going up and down, Dugan slapped it.

"Hey, I never noticed you have a tattoo," said Dugan.

"Birthmark," corrected Cruz. He tensed, waiting for the insult that was sure to come.

But all Dugan said was, "You're a walking Photo 51."

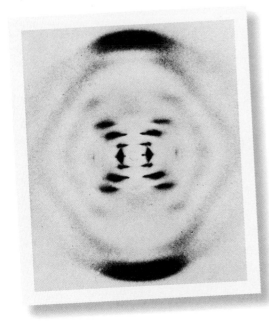

"Huh?"

"Photo 51. It's only the most important photograph *ever* taken." Dugan sat up. "An x-ray image, actually. It was the first to show that human DNA was shaped like a double helix."

Cruz had heard of the pioneering picture but hadn't remembered the number.

"Photo 51 was taken in the 1950s." Professor Luben was towering over them. "A grad student of scientist Rosalind Franklin's used x-ray crystallography techniques that she'd developed." He raised an eyebrow. "Unfortunately, without her knowledge, a colleague showed the image to a couple of competing scientists, Crick and Watson, who used it as a basis for their double-helix model."

"That doesn't seem fair," said Cruz.

"It's not uncommon for one scientist to build on the ideas of another," said their teacher. "That's how we make progress. But in this case, the scales seemed to tip against Dr. Franklin. A decade after the photo was taken, Crick and Watson won the Nobel Prize for their double-helix model. However, Franklin had passed away and could not be considered for the award. History, in the meantime, gave much of the credit for discovering DNA's double-helix shape to Crick and Watson."

"Still seems unfair," said Cruz.

"That must be why the Academy's library is named after Dr. Franklin," said Dugan. "So we'll remember her."

"The school also has an award named in her honor," added their professor. "The Rosalind Franklin award is given to any explorer of any age who contributes to a major scientific breakthrough or discovery."

"I've never heard of it," said Cruz. Dugan was shaking his head, too.

"I don't imagine they've handed out too many," said the professor.

Cruz wondered if Emmett might win it for his Lumagine invention. Could Cruz nominate his friend? He'd have to look into it.

"Hold on." Professor Luben put a hand to his headset. "Guys, the next team is ready to run! Let's get you out of here."

Scrambling to their feet, Cruz and Dugan hurried out of the maze. Officer Dover met them at the main path. "Did you have fun?" she asked.

Cruz looked at Dugan. His teammate wore a gigantic grin. "Yes," said Dugan enthusiastically. "We did."

"Follow me, please." She took them up some steps to another beautiful garden in the park, where their teammates were waiting by a koi pond the size of a swimming pool.

"Great job!" cried Emmett.

"You guys, too. Perfect score." Cruz grinned at Bryndis. "And excellent instructions. I now know my left from my right in Icelandic."

Bryndis smiled back.

"Good run," Sailor said to Dugan.

Instead of his usual I-couldn't-care-less sneer, Dugan said, "Thanks. You guys were great, too."

Cruz saw Sailor jerk back in surprise.

"Let's get something to eat." Emmett had turned and was walking backward toward a tent at the opposite corner of the pond. Under the big red tent, a table had been set up with juices, fruit, crackers, and assorted Spanish cheeses, like buttery manchego and Valdeón, a marbled blue cheese. There were also small finger foods, called tapas: sliced tomatoes with olive oil on toasted bread rounds and lightly fried fritters filled with ham, chicken, or spinach.

"*Croquetas*—yum!" said Cruz, stacking several of the chicken-finger-shaped fritters on his plate. "Aunt Marisol will be sad to miss this." He turned to Sailor and Emmett, who were in line behind him, and whispered, "I have to talk to you."

Emmett tipped his head, as if to say, *Tell us now,* but Cruz knew this wasn't the time or place to share that he had maybe—no, *definitely*—run past Mr. Rook.

"Later." Cruz reached for a small cluster of red grapes. He wanted to talk to Dugan more about why his teammate might have to leave the Academy, but Dugan had wandered off.

They had to wait for nearly an hour before the other teams were finished, but finally all the explorers were together again at the rail overlooking the labyrinth.

"Congratulations!" said Taryn. "Every one of you displayed excellent teamwork skills, and in the end, the times were close. Before Monsieur Legrand reveals the winning team, I'll let Professor Luben tell you about the prize . . . Uh . . . where is he . . . ?" She glanced around the group. "Is he still eating lunch? Professor Luben?"

"Coming! I'll be right there . . ."

Everyone turned, trying to figure out where his voice was coming from.

"Professor Luben?" Taryn called again.

"Down there!" Ali pointed to a spot below them. "I think he's lost in the maze!"

They saw a hand appear from between the hedges. He was! Professor Luben was stuck in the labyrinth. The explorers started snickering.

"I think he needs a spotter," yelled Dugan, which only made them laugh harder.

They waited while Monsieur Legrand coached their teacher out of the puzzle of paths.

Professor Luben joined them at the top of the steps, only slightly out of breath. "My apologies. Guess I zigged when I should have zagged. Anyway, I'm sure you're all anxious to hear about the prize. I am proud to announce that the winning team of today's competition will get"—he paused dramatically—"to choose where we go in the Mediterranean for your first archaeological expedition!"

Really? They would get to choose? Cool!

"Greece, Italy, Egypt, Turkey, Malta—you name it. The choice is yours," said their instructor. "However, I suspect some of you may want to select the country where you've been surveying looting tiles." He shot Cruz a smirk.

Of course! Professor Luben's cryptic message to Dugan and him about winning the competition was becoming clear. It also explained Cruz's conversation with Aunt Marisol before she'd left *Orion*. His aunt had said she couldn't tell him the location of the mystery expedition, that he'd understand once they reached Barcelona. And she was right. Aunt Marisol wouldn't tell Cruz where the expedition would take him because she couldn't. She didn't know.

"You'll select the country, and I'll help you pinpoint a good site," explained their teacher. "Also, the winning team will get to lead the expedition. I wonder where we'll be going!"

Professor Luben's words sinking in, the team members began turning to one another. Twenty-three explorers started talking at once.

Cruz and Dugan motioned for Sailor, Emmett, and Bryndis to huddle up. "Remember the looting tile we found with the circle outlines?" asked Cruz. "Just before we went through the maze, Professor Luben told Dugan and me that it's likely an archaeological site."

Bryndis's mouth dropped. "You mean, we discovered something?"

"That's the good news," said Dugan. "The bad news is nobody knows *what* it is."

"Now is our chance to find out," piped up Emmett. "If we win, we'll go to Turkey and unearth the circles. We'll be famous explorers!"

Sailor thumped him on the shoulder. "*If* we win."

Monsieur Legrand blew his whistle. "Only one team gets the prize, and you can hash it out then. Time for the results." He lifted his clipboard. "In fourth place, with a time of seven minutes and forty-seven seconds, Team Galileo."

Everyone clapped politely. Team Galileo shuffled their feet in disappointment.

"In third place, with a time of six minutes and nineteen seconds, Team Earhart."

More applause. More sad faces.

Sailor dug her fingers into Cruz's upper arm. "It's Magellan or us. Please let it be us. Please let it be us . . ."

Cruz silently took up the chant. His team had so much more at stake than everyone else. They had a site to explore—and not just any site but one *they* had discovered! How many teams could say that? They had to win. They just *had* to.

"First, I should tell you," said Monsieur Legrand, "that the last two teams were separated by only *eight* seconds. That's how close it was between first and second place, so win or lose, you all should be quite proud. And now, with a time of four minutes and fourteen seconds, the *winner* of the Horta Labyrinth Challenge is . . ."

Sailor's fingernails were breaking Cruz's skin, Emmett's glasses resembled yellow-and-green pinwheels in a windstorm, Bryndis looked like she'd been holding her breath underwater too long, and Dugan was clutching his water bottle so hard, Cruz was sure it was going to burst.

". . . Team Magellan!"

ACK IN THEIR CABIN for the night, Emmett plopped into the navy chair opposite Cruz. "I can't believe we lost to Magellan."

"I know," sighed Cruz, glancing up from his tablet. "Did Magellan choose where we're going yet?"

"I don't think it's official, but it's gotta be Egypt—that was their country in the looting tiles assignment."

"Egypt's cool. Maybe we'll find a lost pyramid."

"Yeah," said Emmett, but the thought did little to cheer them up. Everyone on Team Cousteau had their hearts set on going to Turkey to explore *their* site, and now it wasn't going to happen. Someone else was going to make the big discovery that should have been theirs. It wasn't fair.

Cruz called Lani again. He had been trying to reach her for a half hour, but she wasn't picking up. "Come on, Lani," he groaned.

"Are you going to tell her about seeing Mr. Rook?" asked Emmett. Cruz nodded.

"You're sure it was him?"

"Yes." Once the initial shock had worn off, Cruz knew what, or rather, whom he had seen.

"I wonder what he wants—to finish what he started?"

"Maybe, but if he wanted to kill me, he had the perfect opportunity in the maze," reasoned Cruz. He had only seen the former Academy librarian for a moment, but in that fraction of a second, he had not seen anger or vengeance in his eyes. Cruz had a feeling something else was going on. "It was almost like ... like he was trying to tell me, *I'm still around.* Not in a bad way. Not in a good way. Just ... you know ... I'm here."

"Yeah, well, I don't like him being here," clipped Emmett. "You promised Dr. Hightower you'd tell her if Mr. Rook ever showed up again—"

"I did. I sent a message to Dr. H, ship security, and my aunt. I talked to Captain Iskandar, too. I had to let him know we needed to get to Petra."

At that, Emmett's eyes grew. "What's the plan?"

"This weekend, Sailor, you, and I will take a flight from Barcelona to Amman. From there, we'll drive to Petra and search for the cipher. In the meantime, *Orion* will put out into the Mediterranean and head to Turkey. Once we've got the cipher, we're to contact the ship, and Captain Iskandar will send the ship's helicopter for us."

"What about Taryn?"

"Dr. Hightower said she'd handle it." Cruz tapped Lani's icon on his screen again. "She's still not answering."

"Is she online?"

"Uh-huh."

Emmett held out his hand for Cruz's tablet. Cruz gave it to him, though he didn't see how his roommate was going to get through when

he couldn't. Flopping back in the chair, Cruz put a hand to his head. Girls. Emmett began tapping at the touch-screen keyboard. Soon, his lips turned up at the corners.

Cruz knew that grin. He sat up. "What?"

"She's wearing her headset. I've tapped into the video."

"Where is she?"

"Outside. I *think* I can get us into the communications system, too. Give me a couple of seconds…"

Getting up, Cruz pulled his chair so he was sitting elbow to elbow with Emmett and could see Lani's view. The camera was bobbing. Lani's head was down, her eyes on the ground as she picked her way across an uneven grassy field. What was she doing? Playing soccer or baseball? He didn't see or hear anyone around her. Finally, Lani lifted her head, and Cruz saw a row of rusty buildings, sagging smokestacks, and decaying pipes.

He knew exactly where she was. And after she had promised, too!

"Got it," said Emmett. "We're in."

"Leilani Kealoha!" cried Cruz.

"*Arggh!* Tiko, I told you not to yell in my ear—"

"I'm not Tiko, and you broke your word."

The camera froze. "Cruz?"

"Surprise," he said flatly.

The picture went blurry as she spun. "How did you … how are you—"

"Emmett hacked into your headgear. That's *my* explanation. What's yours? You said you would stay away from the abandoned sugar mill."

"Uh … well, I know, but … after I got to thinking about it, I had to come," she sputtered. "In my defense, technically you never specified *which* mill I was supposed to stay away from. There are a couple on the island, you know."

He knew she'd agreed to his terms too easily. "Lani, if Nebula is in there … if you get caught—"

"Nobody's here. Tiko and I did a full surveillance sweep. The place is empty. I'm going in for a quick look. Tiko's back on the main road keeping watch." She began picking her way across the field toward the dilapidated factory once more. "So now that you're here, want to come along? I thought I'd check out the silo for clues. It's the one place where the roof isn't caving in. I'll make it quick."

"You'd better."

A few yards from the silo, Lani ducked to go through a thicket of overgrown bushes. Twenty feet later, she pushed aside the last of the branches. She was under a canopy of trees. The camera took a moment to adjust to the darkness. Lani gently moved a corroded iron gate barely clinging to its post. It squeaked, sending goose bumps down Cruz's arms.

"I don't like this," he said to Emmett, who gave him a rapid nod.

"Almost there," whispered Lani, swiping at a thatch of branches and brambles to reach the door. The camera picked up a glint of silver. "Look! That's a new lock."

The lock was open. Lani slipped it out of the holes, lifted the latch, and slid the heavy bolt to one side. Carefully opening the silo door, she stepped inside. A single ray of afternoon sunlight shining through an opening in the roof gave the place a spooky glow. Lani walked to the center of the cracked cement floor. She did a slow circle, taking in the curved metal walls and the round funnel-shaped roof. They saw nothing else to indicate that anyone had ever been there. No chair. No ropes. No trash.

No clues.

Cruz's heart sank. "There's nothing there."

"Don't rush me," said Lani, her voice echoing. "We've just begun." He saw a beam of light shoot out in front of her and sweep across the room.

"Flashlight," whispered Emmett. "Smart."

"It's more than that," said Lani. "I added an ultra-sensitive thermal imager that measures heat absorptivity, so if anyone has touched anything here within the last twenty-four hours it'll show up on my screen—and here we go." Moving to the perimeter, she knelt next to the curved wall. "I've got a hit."

"Lani, we've got company," said a male voice that wasn't Cruz's or Emmett's.

"Thanks, Tiko," said Lani. "Can you tell who it is?"

"Nope. They came from another entrance."

"There's another entrance?"

"Apparently," said Tiko.

"Copy that," said Lani. "I'll be out in a minute."

"Not in a minute," barked Cruz. "Now."

"Look at this!" Lani's light had found a crevice in the cement. Two crossed knives were stuck, points down, into the large crack. As Lani pulled them out, Cruz saw they were actually plain silverware, a butter knife and a fork. They were bound together in the middle by something. Was that wire? Lani brought them closer, and Cruz's heart skipped. The wire was actually a silver chain—a necklace. Dangling from the middle of the chain were two goldfish, each swimming in a different direction.

"That's my mom's," cried Cruz. "It's the constellation Pisces, you know, the two fish. My dad made it for my mom's birthday. She was a Pisces, born February 22. After Mom died, Dad always wore it. Always. He wouldn't take it off unless—"

They heard the crash of metal.

"Uh-oh." That was Lani.

"Lani, get out of there!" yelled Cruz.

"I'm getting!" She was rushing toward the door. The camera was jostling, the image cutting in and out. They heard quick footsteps. Saw a tall figure. An arm was reaching for Lani. She pulled away. The camera tipped. The flashlight fell. Lani screamed. Cruz's screen went black.

16

►"**WHAT** happened?" Cruz bolted from his chair. "Emmett, can you get her back? Do *something*!"

"I'm trying, I'm trying." Emmett's fingers were a blur.

"Hurry!" Cruz broke out in a cold sweat. Time was critical. Lani might be fierce and stubborn and tough, but she was a little small for her age. She would be no match for the man in the cowboy boots. A helpless feeling washed over him. "We could call my aunt … or 9-1-1. Or Tiko. Yes, call Tiko, Emmett. He's in my contact list. No, 9-1-1 first, then Tiko."

"Okay … wait … you've got a call coming in," cried Emmett. "It's Lani!"

Cruz grabbed his screen and nearly put his fist through it punching the icon. "Lani? Are you there? Are you okay?"

He could see the back wall of the silo but not his best friend. Where was she?

Oh no! Had Nebula kidnapped her, too?

Suddenly, Lani's face appeared. She peered into her phone screen, her headset around her neck. Her eyes were dark pools, and she was breathing hard. "I'm all right, Cruz."

"What's going on? Who grabbed you?"

Grimacing, Lani rotated her phone screen.

Cruz's jaw fell. "*Aunt Marisol?* What are you doing there?"

His aunt's mouth was so tight Cruz couldn't see a speck of pink lipstick. "I was about to ask Leilani the same question."

"She ... uh ... sort of found my secret notebook," sighed Lani, "which I clearly need to hide in a more secret location."

"And, Cruz, I'm more than a little disappointed in you." Aunt Marisol was glaring into the camera. "How long have you known Nebula was behind your dad's disappearance?"

"Uh ..." Cruz shuffled his feet a few times before mumbling, "The day before Halloween. They sent me an email."

"The day I left the ship! Cruz Sebastian, I cannot believe you'd deliberately keep something like that from me when you know how worried I've been—"

"I ... I didn't have a choice. Nebula's note made it clear that if I told *anyone*, they'd kill Dad. What else could I do? I'm sorry, Aunt Marisol ..."

"All right." She raised a hand. "We all know, unfortunately, what Nebula has done and is capable of doing. They will stop at nothing to get what they want." She bit her thumbnail. "And I'm assuming that what they want in exchange for your dad is the cipher pieces and journal."

"Just the cipher," said Cruz. "They didn't ask for the journal. I guess they must think it was destroyed in the ice cave back in Iceland."

"Or maybe they figure getting two pieces is enough to keep anyone from ever completing the formula," interjected Lani.

"They'd be right," said Cruz's aunt. "It's doubtful even the best Synthesis scientists could re-create your mom's formula with only six of the eight sections. Of course, it's frustrating to have to give up what you've all worked so hard to find already, but it can't be helped."

"Actually, we have a plan for that," burst Emmett, his glasses hunter green ovals. "We're going to make—"

Stretching out a foot, Cruz kicked his roommate.

"Ow!" Emmett gave him a what-did-you-do-that-for? scowl.

"Emmett means we're going to make sure we follow Nebula's instructions," said Cruz, his teeth clenched. "I am supposed to be at the spice bazaar in Istanbul on November 14 to hand over the cipher. Alone."

"I don't like the idea of you going by yourself to the drop point," said his aunt.

"They wouldn't try anything in a crowded market," said Lani.

"Don't be so sure."

"I'll have my octopod," insisted Cruz. "And Mell."

"I'd feel better if you had someone looking out for you," said his aunt.

"It's too dangerous. If I do what they say, we'll get Dad back. If I don't…"

There was no need to complete the thought. Folding her arms, his aunt let out an exasperated sigh, and he knew she wasn't going to let the matter go.

"Aunt Marisol, there's something else," said Cruz. "Lani found Mom's Pisces necklace."

"You did?" She turned to Lani. "Where?"

"Here." Lani ran to the far wall. "I dropped it when I heard you coming."

Cruz's aunt followed with the phone in her hand, the camera pointed up. She bent to pick up the two pieces of silverware bound together with the necklace. The utensils formed an X. As the fish swung between her fingers, Cruz saw her face change. Aunt Marisol knew what he knew, that Cruz's dad would never leave the necklace. Unless he had to.

"It's another clue," whispered Lani, "but we don't know what it means. Do you?"

"No. I wish I did." His aunt's voice broke.

Lani placed a gentle hand over Aunt Marisol's. "We'll figure it out."

If Cruz could have, he would have reached right through his tablet and given his best friend the tightest hug possible.

Aunt Marisol touched her head. "It's starting to rain. We should get out of here. After all, we *are* trespassing. Cruz, I'll call you tomorrow and we'll discuss everything, including Malcolm Rook. Your note was quite a shock, considering he is supposed to be in jail. Please watch your step." She tried to grin. "*Te quiero.*"

"Love you back," he said. "You be careful, too."

After hanging up, he set his tablet on his starry night desk. Emmett had pulled down one of his sloth socks and was rubbing his ankle.

"Sorry about that." Cruz scrunched his nose. "But I knew you were going to tell my aunt about the decoy cipher."

"So?"

"I didn't want her to know."

"Why not?"

"She would have tried to talk me out of it. She would have said, *Suppose Nebula is one step ahead of you. What if they already know what it looks like? Is that a chance you're willing to take?* She would have said it was too risky."

"But you don't have a choice—"

"Yes, I do." Cruz let out a shallow breath. "The cipher may have been my mother's most important accomplishment, but nothing is more important than my dad's life. I'll make a copy of the cipher—an exact copy—for me to keep, but I'm giving the real stones to Nebula."

"Cruz, there's a reason your mom didn't make copies. Let's think about this—"

"That's all I've been doing—thinking and thinking and thinking. I'm done thinking, Emmett. I've made up my mind."

His roommate opened his mouth but then slowly closed it. Emmett dipped his head, the color of his frames changing from hunter green to pale blue.

Acceptance.

THE NEXT AFTERNOON, Cruz was wandering down *Orion*'s explorers' passage alone. He was so deep in thought, pondering his mom's clue about what kind of animal would be at home both in the clouds and under the sea, that he almost didn't hear his name.

Almost.

Cruz stopped. Took four steps back. Turning his head to peer into the cabin, he put a hand to his chest.

"Yes, you." From her rocking chair, Taryn waved a crochet hook. "Got a sec?"

Cruz went toward her. He didn't know how she managed to glide forward and back in that rocker while the ship was gently rocking side to side and not throw up. Cruz loved being on the water, but even he had a feeling that if he tried that he wouldn't be able to keep his lunch from reappearing.

"Close the door," said Taryn.

Meekly, Cruz obeyed. "Am I in trouble?"

She gazed up at him with a smirk. "Do I look like you're in trouble?"

"No, but..." He didn't finish the rest of the sentence running through his brain, which was *I'm never quite sure with you.* Cruz plopped down next to Hubbard, who was stretched out in his dog bed, fast asleep.

Taryn went back to her crocheting. Whatever she was making was a light-seagull-gray color, very thick, and quite large—probably a blanket.

Cruz ran his fingers through the short, soft fur on Hubbard's neck. The sleeping dog let out a contented sigh.

"Any news about your dad?" asked Taryn.

Cruz tensed. Taryn knew his father was missing, but like most everyone else on board, she had no clue about the circumstances surrounding his disappearance. "No," he said quietly.

"I'm so sorry. I only met him once, but I could see right away how devoted he was to you. It must be hard to soldier on. I know the two of you talked to each other quite a bit."

Cruz felt his throat closing up. He had been trying not to think about that. After a very long minute, he managed to squeak out, "We did."

A hand was on his shoulder. "I know. I mean, I don't *really* know, but I can imagine . . ."

Cruz glanced up at his adviser. "Even though you're, like . . . old . . . don't you talk to your parents? Don't you miss them?"

"I'm not *that* old." She twisted her lips. "And my parents are gone."

"Oh. Sorry."

"It's okay," soothed Taryn. "I'm not alone. I have a family. A big one. Twenty-three kids, to be exact."

That made him grin. She was talking about the explorers, of course.

"I worry about every single one of them. Are they homesick or lonely? Are they studying too hard or not hard enough? Are they sleeping soundly in their own beds?" She cleared her throat. "Or in the ship's greenhouse?"

Cruz's mouth fell open. "You knew? But how—?"

She shifted her eyebrows. "I have my ways."

"So I guess I'm in trouble *now*."

"You ought to be." Taryn slid the crochet hook through several big loops, wound a strand of yarn over the hook, and pulled it through all the loops. She did the same move three more times. He knew she was keeping him in suspense on purpose. His dad used to do the same trick when he was deciding if and how to punish him. "But . . . I suppose we all need to break the rules once in a while, and if hanging out with veggies for a night with your friends is your idea of fun, I guess I could let it slide this once."

He relaxed. "Thanks, Taryn."

"*This once.*" She eyed him over the blanket. "Next time, ask permission."

"You would have said yes?"

"No! It's a hard floor in a hot greenhouse. You belong in your own bed."

Cruz rolled his eyes. Naturally, she saw him.

"Eye rolling is also forbidden," said Taryn. "Read your student handbook."

He chuckled. Two months into the school year and Cruz still hadn't gotten around to that little chore.

"I had an interesting chat with Dr. Hightower this morning," said his adviser.

Cruz tried pretending he didn't already know what she was about to say. "Yeah?"

"She says she is sending Emmett, Sailor, and you on a short Academy mission this weekend. Wouldn't tell me what it was for or where you were going, just that she was sending the school's jet to Barcelona and I was to make sure that the three of you were at the airport by five a.m. tomorrow."

"Oh . . . really? A . . . a . . . a mission? The . . . the three of us? I'm sure she'll tell us what it's all about soon." Cruz cringed at his bad acting.

It was Taryn's turn to roll her eyes. Setting her blanket and yarn in the basket next to her chair, she bent forward. "Look, I know your life is . . . complicated. I don't know how or why. The details aren't important. What *is* important is you. The only thing you need to know is there isn't anything I wouldn't do to keep you safe." Vivid green eyes pierced his. "Got it?"

Cruz didn't doubt she was serious. From the moment Taryn Secliff had welcomed him to the Academy, she had been clear and consistent in her guidance. He sensed an honesty about her, that she would never steer him wrong. And although he knew he couldn't trust anyone, Cruz wanted to trust her. "Got it," he said.

"Good. Wherever you are tomorrow night, do me a favor and call me, okay? I won't be able to sleep unless I know you're all right."

Cruz promised he would.

"Thanks." Picking up her crochet work again, Taryn glanced at the old-fashioned clock next to her made of exposed gears inside a glass dome. "Now if you'll excuse me, I have approximately seven more minutes of blissful me time before I have to give two explorers from Team Earhart a lecture about the importance of tidiness."

Cruz gave Hubbard one last pet and got to his feet.

He heard her rocker squeak. "A word to the wise?"

"Yeah?"

"Never play poker."

Cruz couldn't stop grinning all the way back to his cabin. Taryn was right, as usual. He never had been much good at lying.

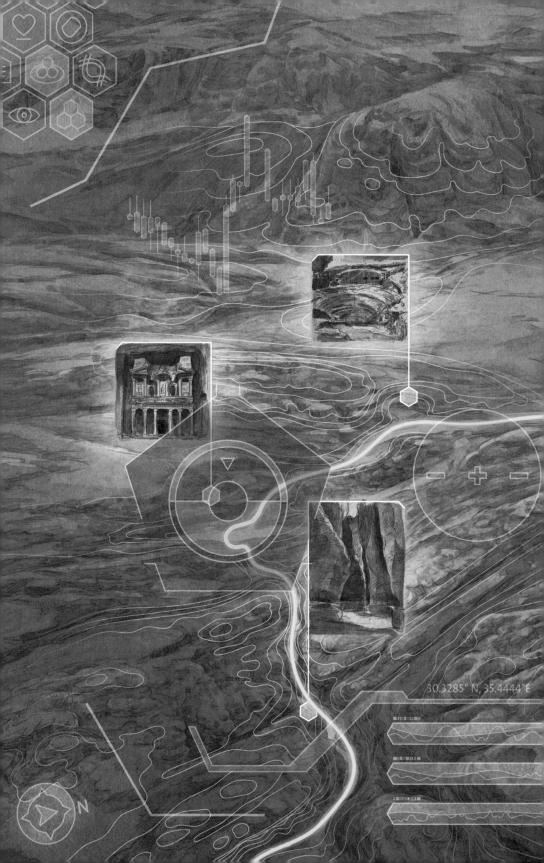

30.3285° N, 35.4444° E

LEBANON
Mediterranean
Sea
SYRIA
ISRAEL
WEST
BANK
IRAQ
GAZA STRIP
PETRA,
JORDAN
JORDAN
EGYPT
SAUDI ARABIA

►SETTING ONE FOOT onto

gray paver stones warmed by the desert sun, Cruz unfolded himself
from the Autonomous Auto. His butt was numb. His neck was stiff. And
his tongue felt like sandpaper. The flight from Barcelona to Amman on
Condor, the Academy's jet, had been smooth but long—four hours. After
that, it was another three-hour drive down the Desert Highway from
Amman to Wadi Musa crammed in a mini Auto Auto with broken climate
controls, windshield wipers that clicked on at will, and a certain bottom-
less pit of a roommate who had to stop for snacks every 20 minutes. At
least it was warm in Wadi Musa, the modern town built on the outskirts
of the ancient city of Petra—hot, actually. *Condor*'s pilot had told them
that the temperatures in Jordan were unseasonably warm for late fall.
It should have been around 65 degrees but was close to 80.

Sailor tucked her ponytail into her safari hat. "This is different from
what I was expecting."

Taking a swig from his water bottle, Cruz agreed. He had anticipated exploring a fairly remote desert location, but this was more like
a theme park! Tourists swarmed around them, heading in from nearby
hotels, restaurants, and parking lots down a stone gateway lined with
flags. A sign above the main archway read WELCOME TO PETRA. Cruz, Sailor,
and Emmett grabbed their backpacks from the trunk.

Cruz glanced down at his OS band. It was 10 minutes after two o'clock. He had hoped to arrive by one, but Emmett's snack stops had put them behind. They now had less than 24 hours to locate the cipher.

"I'd like to give you more time, but I'm afraid I can't, Cruz," Dr. Hightower had explained. She'd called just before bedtime last night to tell him she'd arranged for a hotel so they could stay overnight near Petra. "You must be in class on Monday morning like everyone else or your professors are going to want to know why you're not. As it is, I'm sure some of your classmates are going to be wondering where you've disappeared to over the weekend, as well. If they ask, tell them you accompanied Captain Iskandar ashore to make some presentations about applying to the Academy. We often ask current explorers to share their experiences with prospective students. The captain will cover for you, if necessary."

"Okay," said Cruz.

"You'll have to leave Petra by no later than noon Sunday to make it back to the ship by curfew." A fluff of white hair loomed closer to the camera. "No later, Cruz."

"I understand, Dr. Hightower. Noon, Sunday."

The edges of her mouth softened. "Good luck, explorer."

"Thank you." He tried to keep the worry he felt from creeping into his voice.

He hoped it was enough time.

Throwing his backpack over one shoulder, Cruz followed Emmett and Sailor and the rest of the crowd under the welcome arch and into a large circular courtyard. The open area was rimmed by a visitor center, a food court, and souvenir shops. People milled about, eating and drinking, inspecting the hanging T-shirts and spinning the racks of postcards. The trio headed down a brick walkway, purchased their tickets, and passed through the main gates.

Cruz slid his GPS sunglasses down onto his nose and tapped the globe pin on his lapel. "Map of Petra, Jordan, please." Instantly, an opaque diagram of the ancient city appeared in front of his eyes. It self-adjusted in the sunlight so that Cruz was able to easily see the virtual map, as well as the real trail in front of him.

Sailor and Emmett did the same. On the long trip in that morning, they had come up with a plan. Petra was a big place with dozens of landmarks, so they would start their search for the cipher with the most well-known sites: a tomb called the Treasury, the Nabataean amphitheater, the Byzantine church, and the Great Temple. If they didn't find the stone piece in any of these spots, they would expand their quest.

Cruz studied the map in his glasses. To reach the main city of Petra, they would have to first walk about a half mile through the scrubland valley to the Siq, a narrow, rocky canyon. The Siq was about three-quarters of a mile long. Once they navigated the ravine, they would reach the main city of Petra, which was about a mile in length. There were also several sites located in the rocky cliffs above the Siq and the town's ruins, if you were willing to hike up to reach them. Standing here, seeing Petra laid out in front of him, Cruz's heart skipped. They had less than two hours before the place closed today and another six hours tomorrow to find the cipher piece.

Cruz motioned for his friends to huddle up. "We'll stick to the plan. The Treasury is at the end of the Siq," he said quietly. "If what we're looking for isn't there, we'll go into the city. Most of the major sites are located there."

"I didn't realize there were so many places to search." Sailor shook her head. "The Urn Tomb, the Palace Tomb, Winged Lions Temple, Ridge Church—"

Emmett picked up the list. "The Silk Tomb, the Corinthian Tomb—"

"Then I guess we'd better get started," clipped Cruz.

They couldn't afford to waste even a minute.

The explorers fell in step with the stream of tourists heading down a wide dirt road. As they wound their way through the valley, the low scrubland hills gave way to massive boulders and flat-topped stony outcrops. The peachy rock face had been sculpted into monolithic shapes and, in many places, bore the scars of holes—tombs. Hundreds of them. Cruz hoped his mom hadn't hidden the cipher in some small, out-of-the-way tomb, because if she had, it would take him years to find it.

At the half-mile mark, they reached a stone dam. It had been built across the entrance to the Siq and, according to the signs, rebuilt over the years to keep flash floods from reaching the heart of Petra. The narrow gorge that was the Siq was paved with huge stone slabs. Slowly spinning on his heel to walk backward on the flagstone, Cruz gazed up at the mammoth, ruddy red walls of stone closing in around them. His GPS readout revealed that the Siq was a crack in the mountain formed by a natural geologic fault in the Earth and that, in some places, the gap was less than 10 feet wide.

"The walls are six hundred feet high in some spots!" cried Sailor, who was reading the same information in her own GPS glasses. She was craning her neck, too.

Cruz believed it. He could barely see a sliver of blue sky.

"A little claustrophobic," said Emmett, his shoulder bumping stone.

Seeing the long shadows darkening their path, Cruz picked up the pace to a brisk walk. They wove between the snakelike channels the Nabataeans had cut into the sides of the Siq at ground level. These channels, along with underground tunnels and reservoirs, had once supplied Petra with freshwater. With its horizontal layers of pink and red rock, twisted stone arches, and wavy walls smoothed by humans, water, and time, the canyon was a work of art. Every turn brought something new to see: more tombs, carved animals, and baetyls—sacred stones that were contained in niches. The explorer in Cruz longed to stop for a closer look at these wonders, but he knew they couldn't. Now and again, voices would echo through the crevasse to remind them that hikers were above, heading to points high in the cliffs.

Even though they were now mostly in the shade, there was little wind to cool them. Cruz's feet were steaming. He hated having hot feet. It seemed as if they had been walking forever. Rounding yet another curve, Cruz reached for the bandanna in his back pants pocket to wipe the sweat from his brow. When he took the cloth away, he was facing a Greek-style temple carved into the side of a cliff. It was as tall as a sky-scraper!

The Treasury!

"Al-Khazneh," gushed Emmett.

As they gawked, a written description of the temple appeared in their sunglasses.

With its Corinthian columns, sculptures of gods and Amazons, and ornate carvings of eagles, griffins, vases, and rosettes, Al-Khazneh, or the Treasury, is one of Petra's most elaborate human-made wonders. Although the 128-foot monument contains no inscription, archaeologists believe it was a royal tomb made, perhaps, for Aretas IV, a successful Nabataean king who ruled Petra from 9 B.C. to A.D. 40. The name Khazneh means "treasure," because legend foretold that riches were hidden there. No such wealth was ever found.

"It's a perfect hiding spot," Sailor whispered to him. "It has to be here."

Ever since he'd seen a photo of the tomb, Cruz had thought so, too. However, a row of chains attached to metal poles blocked the front steps. No one was allowed beyond that point.

"We can't go in," said Emmett. "It's not open to the public."

Sailor snorted. "We're not going to let that stop us, are we?"

Cruz watched the tourists hovering around the steps to the tomb. A tall teen girl with long wheat blond hair in a red tee and jeans with a white jacket tied around her waist was taking a selfie with the Treasury behind her. There must have been at least 50 others in the gorge doing the same thing. Cruz turned. Directly across from the Treasury was a long open tent—a gift shop and a food stand. There were outdoor tables and even vending machines. "Oh, yeah, I'll just slip in," said Cruz. "No one will notice."

"We need a diversion," said Sailor, as if it were the easiest thing in the world.

Cruz cocked an eyebrow. "Like?"

"Heatstroke," Emmett said so quickly Cruz wasn't sure he'd heard his friend correctly.

"Huh?"

"Heatstroke," echoed Sailor. "Sweet as. Ready?"

Before Cruz could say he was definitely *not* ready, she'd put a hand to her forehead and collapsed onto the sand.

"Uh … help?" squeaked Emmett.

"Louder," Sailor mumbled out of the side of her mouth.

"Help!"

"Oh, brother." Cruz rolled his eyes. This was never going to work.

Except it was working. People were hurrying toward them. Emmett smacked Cruz on the arm with the back of his hand. *Go!*

Like a fish swimming upstream, Cruz ducked through the crowd and took off across the canyon floor. Pushing himself up onto the stone platform in front of the Treasury, he hopped over the chains. Cruz scrambled up the steps and through the middle of six columns protecting the massive rectangular opening. Once inside, Cruz swung right and flattened himself against a stone wall. It took a minute for his breath to slow and his heart to beat normally again.

Cruz flipped up his sunglasses, his eyes traveling over the vivid red, white, pink, and gold layers of rock. The colors swirled and blended together like streamers in a breeze. The tomb was much smaller than he'd expected: a square of less than 15 feet to the back wall and 15 feet from one side to the other. Each wall had a door-like opening and a couple of small steps leading up to it. Staying close to the wall, Cruz moved from one door to the next, peering inside. Every door led to a small inlet—burial crypts. Dead ends. His eyes darting across the floor, then up and over the ceiling, Cruz took one last good look around. It was nothing but stone. Stone and more stone.

No confetti. No mythical creature. No reward.

Cruz leaned to peer out the main entrance. The excitement over, tourists were strolling back toward the tomb. It was now or never. With one deep breath, Cruz dashed out of the tomb. A few people looked at him with disapproval as he hurdled the chains, but nobody said anything. He spotted his friends on the far wall of the canyon next to the gift shop. Sailor and Emmett were standing under an outcrop. Sailor was sipping water. A thin, dark-haired, bearded man in a white shirt and khakis was kneeling next to her. As Cruz approached, he heard her say, "Thank you. I'm feeling better now."

"Be sure to keep drinking," said the man, rising. "It's easy to get dehydrated out here."

"I will. Thanks again."

When the man left, Sailor and Emmett bent toward Cruz. "Well?"

"It's not there."

Sailor blew out a big puff of air. "Dang!"

"One site down," said Emmett. "A whole lot more to go."

They continued through the canyon and, in another hundred yards or so, the rosy stone walls began to part. In Cruz's glasses, his GPS indicated the path had a name: the Street of Facades. Sites began popping up in front of their eyes: the Tomb of Unayshu, the Nabataean Theater, the Palace Tomb, the Silk Tomb, public restrooms, Triclinium, Nymphaeum, the Great Temple, the Byzantine church...

"Whoa!" said Emmett. "I guess there wasn't room on our display to show us everything when we first came in."

"At least we can rule out the restrooms," muttered Sailor.

There were so many sites! Cruz wondered if they should split up. They could cover more territory that way.

Emmett pointed ahead. "There's the amphitheater, our second site on the list."

To their left was a row of crumbling columns. Behind the pillars, a semicircle of hundreds of sculpted stone seats shadowed a stage. The explorers' GPS glasses revealed that the theater was carved completely out of the cliff and could seat 8,500 people. Also, it had been badly damaged by repeated floods, as well as a major earthquake in the first century A.D.

Emmett was trotting toward the theater. Behind Cruz, however, Sailor had stopped. He turned. She put her hands on her hips.

"What's wrong?" asked Cruz impatiently. His feet were roasting. He was thirsty. He was starting to get hungry, too.

"I don't know."

Cruz flipped up his sunglasses. "Do you want to split up?"

"No," she sighed. "I was thinking … I mean, it seems to me—"

"Hey!" Emmett was returning. "Are you guys coming or what?"

Sailor took off her safari hat and wiped her damp forehead with the back of her hand. With his sunglasses off, Cruz noticed that her cheeks were red. Her neck was a splotchy red, too.

"I could use a break," said Cruz. Glancing around, he pointed to yet another one of the many open-air gift shop/food stands they'd passed along their route. "There."

Once under the flat cream canopy, they chose a table near a rack of postcards as far from the cashier as possible. There were no other tourists in the seating area. Cruz let his pack fall from his shoulders. *Ahhhh.* It felt great to be free of the weight. It was also a good 10 degrees cooler in the shade. Cruz took out a bottle of sunscreen, sprayed some on his arms, and handed it to Sailor. Reaching into his pack, Emmett brought out three oranges. He rolled one to Cruz across the table and handed the other to Sailor, who was beside him.

The girl in the red tee and jeans was walking past. She was wearing her white jacket now and carrying a paper map. She did not look their way.

Cruz started to peel his orange, his gaze absently drifting to the postcard rack behind Emmett's shoulder. Its long, neat rows were stocked with color photographs of Petra's various sites, like the Siq, the Treasury, and the Great Temple. Cruz tipped his head. One of the postcards had a photo of mosaic artwork. The way the tiles were done, in a twisted rope pattern … it kind of looked like …

He glanced at his wrist.

Nah! He was imagining it.

"Sorry I hung us up." Sailor punctured the rind of her orange with her thumbnail. "I know you wanted to stick to the plan and everything, Cruz, but I just keep thinking your mom wouldn't have hidden the cipher in a place where it could get buried or lost …"

"Like the amphitheater?" prompted Cruz.

She nodded. "Also, so far, it seems like your mom isn't hiding the pieces just *anywhere*. I mean, she put the first piece of the cipher in the base of your holo-dome and the second one in a packet of seeds with a label that had her favorite song on it—both things that meant something personal to you."

"I get it," said Emmett. "You're saying that somewhere in Petra is a spot that will link Cruz to his mother."

"Exactly." She glanced at Cruz. "A place that will make sense to you and only you."

"The question is, where?" Emmett drummed the table with his fingertips.

Cruz put a slice of orange into his mouth, enjoying the burst of stringy tartness on his tongue. His eyes kept returning to the mosaic art on the postcard. Cruz squinted to read the caption: *The Byzantine Church.*

"I think we're on the right track," Sailor was saying. "I mean, I think your mom would pick one of the major sites, but maybe we can rule some out."

"I agree," said Emmett. "What if we pulled up close-up photos of the more protected places on our GPS? Cruz could study them and see if they trigger anything, like a favorite thing or a memory."

"Good idea," said Sailor. "That would keep us from running all over the place."

Leaning over, Cruz reached past Emmett's shoulder to pluck the postcard from its holder. Upon closer examination,

he could see that stone walls surrounded the mosaic artwork—ah, it was a floor! Hundreds of tiny, dark glass tiles had been arranged in circles and squares. Inside each shape was a scene—animal, person, vase, plant—on a white-tile background. The entire grid was framed by black and white tiles set in a twisted rope design that looked similar to his birthmark. Placing the postcard on the table between the three of them, Cruz set his left forearm next to the photo, turning his wrist up. "Is this what you mean about finding something that makes sense to me?"

His friends glanced down at the postcard. Emmett and Sailor slowly removed their sunglasses, their eyes moving from the picture to Cruz's wrist and back to the card again. The patterns weren't identical. But they were close. Awfully close.

Cruz's lips turned up. "Well?"

His friends were grinning, too.

"Maybe one of these animals is at home in the clouds and under the sea," whispered Emmett.

Cruz bobbed his head. That was what he was thinking, too.

Sailor tipped her head. "Guys, is it me or do all those colorful tiles look a little like"—she hesitated, wincing the way you do when you aren't sure you have the right answer to a question—"confetti?"

Cruz's jaw fell. He had never thought of that, but now it was all he *could* think of. It was so obvious! The double-helix pattern. The mosaic animal tiles. They could lead to only one conclusion: The cipher was in the Byzantine church.

Cruz jumped up, nearly knocking over the table. "Let's go!"

18

THROWING BACK their chairs,
the three explorers grabbed their packs, tossed their orange rinds into
the compost bin, and raced back to the main path. A few hundred feet
beyond the amphitheater, the sandy road widened and the sun revealed
Petra's hilly scrubland and flat-topped boulders. They jogged past the
crumbling foundations of ancient temples, tombs, and buildings. Following their GPS, they veered right off the main street and headed up
a rocky trail to reach the Byzantine church at the top of the hill.

The roof of the structure was long gone, replaced by a white canvas
tent supported by metal beams. The explorers darted through the
ruins of the church's outer stone atrium—Cruz first, then Emmett,
then Sailor—under the tent and into the temple. Two rows of broken
columns divided the church into three sections. The floor of the center
aisle was made of smooth, flat stone, but the two outside aisles were
composed of the mosaics they had seen on the postcard. Cruz's GPS
flashed that the sanctuary was 85 feet long by 50 feet wide and each
of the side aisles was paved with 753 square feet of mosaics—information Cruz appreciated but didn't need to know at this moment. "GPS
off," he ordered.

Thankfully, the church wasn't crowded—only a young couple carrying a baby and a small group of elderly tourists wearing pastel floral
shirts and straw hats.

"I'll take the right side," huffed Cruz.

"We'll go left," said Emmett, grabbing Sailor's hand.

Again, barriers had been set up to prevent anyone from walking on the delicate tiles. However, instead of chains or ropes, these barricades were made of wooden slats anchored to heavy posts. Cruz, Emmett, and Sailor had to lean over the wood fences to glimpse the artwork on the floor. On Cruz's side, there were three rows running lengthwise, and each row had about 20 scenes. The spiral pattern that matched his birthmark framed the entire section. Cruz quickly scanned each of the illustrations. Unfortunately, some of the mosaics were missing many of their tiles, making it nearly impossible to tell what the original picture had been. Cruz ticked the animals off in his head as he hurried from one row to the next.

Donkey, bird, plant.

Horse, buffalo, woman carrying a fish.

Salamander, duck, eagle.

Cruz stopped.

He backtracked to the first row, located above the outer spiral mosaic frame. Cruz knelt next to a stump of a column and looked through the slats of the barrier. The salamander in the square frame had no legs. However, it *did* have a sleek body, fins, and a tail. Like a fish. It also had round eyes, a head crest, and a beak. Like a bird.

This had to be it!

"Emmett! Sailor!" he hissed.

They flew across the church.

"At home both in the clouds and under the sea," whispered Sailor.

Emmett slapped Cruz's shoulder. "It's a fird, a combination bird and fish."

Sailor chuckled. "Or a birsh."

"It must be under the mosaic," said Cruz softly. "Remember, Mom said, 'if you're willing to reach out, you'll have your reward.'"

They understood. Cruz was supposed to touch the mosaic. Unfortunately, the barriers made it clear no one was supposed to touch anything. The trio casually glanced around.

The group of elderly tourists was leaving. When the couple with the baby turned to walk down the aisle on the opposite side of the church, Cruz slipped an arm under the lowest wooden slat of the barrier. The tiny glass stones felt cool and gritty under his fingertips. Patting the floor, he felt for loose tiles. Nothing. He tried to wedge a fingernail under them. He covered the whole mosaic, but not a single tile moved.

"Be sure to check them all." Emmett was on his toes, peering over the top of the barrier.

Cruz grunted, his cheek smooshed against the wood. "I am."

"Check the spiral frame, too," reminded Sailor.

Cruz stuck his other hand under the barrier, his fingers gliding over the twisted rope mosaic flowing past the salamander's belly. Everything was solid.

"Uh ... Cruz?" Sailor said softly.

"Wait a second. I'll try farther down the frame." Flattening himself onto his belly, Cruz was able to extend his reach.

"Cruz?"

"One sec." He strained, wiggling his fingers to gain a few more inches.

"Cruz!"

"What?" He turned his head.

A pair of black zip boots was inches from his nose. His eyes traveled slowly up, over a pair of straight black pants to a black high-collar shirt to the grim face of a man about his dad's age. Dark eyes turned to slits. It was one of the tour group guides. He was crooking his finger at Cruz. Behind him stood a sheepish Emmett and Sailor, their eyes down, their hands clasped.

"Uh ... hi," Cruz said lightly, going up on his knees. "We're from Explorer Academy, and we were, you know ... exploring."

"Yes, well, from now on, please explore from *behind* the barricades. If one of the security guards catches you ..." He shook his head.

"Sorry."

"It's almost four o'clock," said the guide. "We'll be closing soon anyway, so you should start back to the main entrance now. The sun goes down behind the hills at four thirty, and you do not want to get caught in here after dark. There are no lights in Petra."

"We will. Thanks." Cruz stood and brushed sand from the knees of his pants.

Picking up his pack, he shuffled toward the doorway. Emmett and Sailor joined him, one on each side. The three of them exchanged worried looks. There was nothing they could do. They had to leave. The tour guide was watching.

"What now?" hissed Emmett as they made their way down the hill.

"I don't know," sighed Cruz. "Maybe we had the wrong mosaic. Or the wrong place? I don't know."

He had been so sure they'd find the cipher. Where had they gone wrong?

Sailor slung an arm around Cruz's shoulder. "We'll come back tomorrow. We'll try again."

Swallowing a lump, he nodded. What else could they do?

As the sun slipped low in the sky, the explorers followed the rest of the tourists heading for the exit. They were disappointed and tired and hungry. They walked quickly. No one spoke. With the deepening of the evening shadows, the walls of the Siq seemed even tighter and taller than when they had come through the first time. The surrounding rock magnified the voices and laughter of the hikers descending the cliff trails. The explorers were past the Treasury when Emmett stopped in his tracks. "Uh-oh."

Cruz glanced at him. "What?"

He grimaced. "I think I left my GPS glasses in the Byzantine church."

Sailor and Cruz groaned. They watched as their friend rummaged through his backpack.

"They're not here." Emmett shook his head. "Taryn's gonna kill me if I lose those. I have to go back. Can you guys watch my pack? I'll run faster without it." He backed away. "Or go on ahead, if you want. I'll catch up ..."

"Emmett, no! We should all stay together." Cruz tossed Emmett's pack onto his free shoulder. Immediately, he sagged under the weight of it. Geez, what did Emmett have in there anyway?

"I'll go with him," said Sailor. "You stay and watch our stuff." She wriggled out of her pack and dropped it at Cruz's feet. "We won't be long."

"That'll give me a chance to call Taryn," said Cruz. "I promised I'd check in."

He watched Sailor vanish around the corner. Cruz swept their backpacks to the side of the narrow passage so no one would trip over them, before taking off his own pack to add to the pile. Leaning against the curved stone wall, Cruz drank some water. The number of tourists was dwindling. He made the call to Taryn.

"Everything okay?" she asked. "You sound beat."

"Never better," he said, even though he knew she would see through the lie. "How's Hubbard?"

"Missing you. He's not the only one."

"We'll be back tomorrow night on schedule."

"Okay. In the meantime, be sure and let me know if you need anything."

"I will."

"And be careful."

"Of what?" he asked, trying to sound like he was doing nothing more than hanging out with his friends.

"Knowing you, I'd say everything."

Snickering, Cruz said goodbye. He wanted to call Lani or his aunt, except it was 3 a.m. back home.

Bored with waiting, he dug his mind-control camera out of his pack. Cruz placed the lightweight, flat metal strip on his head. He popped the lens down over his right eye to turn the camera on. All he had to do to take a picture was think the word "photo" and shut his eyes. The camera would sync up with his brain waves and do the rest. First, Cruz took a few shots of the canyon walls. Stepping into the center of the thin path, he tilted his head back. Above the ravine walls, he saw a wedge of twilight. The sky was turning a deep rose orange. Aunt Marisol would love this. Lani, too.

Photo.

He spun the other way, his head still back, to get a different angle.
Photo.

Cruz saw something move overhead. Was it a plane? It seemed to be getting closer—almost falling. He heard a scream.

"Rocks!"

19

CRUZ was suddenly rolling.

Everything was a blur. He heard thunder. Saw red. Tasted sand. When at last his body tumbled to a stop, Cruz was on his back, his left leg bent under him. A cloud of dust was settling. His lungs burned. His back hurt. Something was weighing him down. He felt a swish across his neck. The weight lifted. A face appeared. It was her—the girl he'd seen at the Treasury and at the roadside stand.

Blue-gray eyes peered through a tangle of blond hair. "You okay?"

He coughed. "I . . . I think so."

She pushed her hair back and crawled backward to rest on her knees. "That was close."

Unwrapping his legs, Cruz sat up. It felt like he'd been punched in the side. Hard.

"Sorry 'bout that." The girl was brushing sand from her top. "I had to sort of . . . tackle you to get you out of the path of the falling rocks." She had an accent similar to that of Weatherly Bright, one of the explorers, who was from England.

"Seriously?" He rubbed his waist. "You . . . you pushed me out of the way?"

"It was either that or watch you become a pancake."

Cruz surveyed the debris that surrounded him—pebbles, stones, and a couple of larger bowling-ball-size boulders. His eyes traveled up

the never-ending canyon walls, now painted a cherry red by the fading light. He heard no one in the cliffs above, but his mind rushed to one conclusion: Nebula. He pushed the thought away. They wouldn't go so far as to follow him here, would they? Dumb question. Of course they would.

Standing, the girl swept the sand from her jeans, then held out a hand to Cruz. He took it and got to his feet. He picked up his mind-control camera, which had been knocked clean off of him. Cruz hoped it wasn't broken.

She glanced around. "Weren't you with some friends?"

"Uh, yeah. One of them forgot something . . . back in Petra."

"Well, they'd better hurry. It's almost the end of the day, and once the sun goes down, it's pitch-black in here."

"I'm sure they'll be back any—"

What had she just said?

Of course! How could he have forgotten his mom's clue: *It may seem like a strange mythical creature, but* at the end of the day, *if you're willing to reach out, you'll have your reward.*

They *had* been at the right place, just not at the right time. Cruz was supposed to be at the Byzantine church at sunset. It had to be close to sunset now!

The girl was studying him. "Are you sure you didn't bonk your head?"

"No . . . I mean, yes . . . Sorry, I've got to go." He ran for the backpacks. Cruz flung Emmett's pack on his left shoulder, Sailor's on his right, and, clutching his own pack to his chest, turned back toward Petra. "Thanks again . . . who are you?"

She walked backward away from him. "Does it matter? Be careful, okay? I can't always be around to save your neck from Nebula."

Stunned, Cruz dropped his backpack. "Wait!" he called, but she had turned. She slipped into the thin gap between the rock walls and was gone.

He couldn't go after her. Juggling all three of their packs, Cruz headed toward Petra. At the amphitheater, he met his friends coming the other way. "We have … to go back … to the church," gasped Cruz.

"Again?" moaned Emmett. "Why?"

"Rocks fell … girl saved me … I'll explain later, but I … we … forgot the rest of the clue. We were supposed to be at the church … at the end of the day."

"The clue! The end of the day!" Sailor was putting it together now. "Uh-oh. The tour guide said the sun sets at four thirty."

Emmett checked his OS band. "It's four eighteen now."

"That gives us twelve minutes," gulped Cruz. "If we hurry, we might be able to make it."

Everyone grabbed a pack, and they took off at full speed down the Street of Facades and up the hill to the Byzantine church. Halfway up the slope, Emmett stopped. He fell forward at the waist, his hands on his knees. "You guys go ahead … I can't …"

"Oh yes you can," said Cruz, grabbing Emmett's heavy pack.

Sailor grabbed Emmett.

They made it to the church ruins as the sun was dipping behind the hills. The sanctuary was empty. Dropping their backpacks at the entrance, the trio raced across the church to the half columns and wooden barricades protecting the mosaic floor. His sides aching, Cruz fell to his knees beside the broken stone column in front of the bird-fish mosaic. He flung his arms under the slats of the barricade. Cruz slapped his left palm onto the tiles of the bird-fish and his right hand onto the twisting pattern of tiles beside it—just to cover all his bases. "Okay, Mom, I'm reaching out," he huffed. "What time is it?"

"Four twenty-eight," croaked Emmett.

Cruz's chest was heaving. His brain was reeling. He clamped his eyes shut. He hoped this would work. This was the only sunset they were going to get in Petra, his only shot at finding the cipher. Cruz could hear his heartbeat thumping in his head. *Ba-bump. Ba-bump. Ba-bump.*

His right cheek felt warm. Cruz opened his eyes. A ray of light was shining through a small hole in the front stone wall of the church. The sunbeam shot across the length of the mosaic floor and was broken only by Cruz's head. He pulled his neck back a few inches so it wouldn't blind him, and the sun hit the column. In the golden light, Cruz saw something on the column he hadn't seen before: a hairline crack. The fracture went down and across the pillar, forming a rectangular shape. It made four perfect sides—maybe a little too perfect. What had Professor Luben taught them? He'd said nature was random. Abstract. Unique. Only humans were precise.

If that was true . . .

"Four twenty-nine," announced Emmett.

A drawer! It had to be a secret drawer! If Cruz hadn't been kneeling with his hands placed just so on the floor, he would never have seen it. He also knew that if he lifted his hands, he would no longer be reaching out to the bird-fish, as the clue had instructed. "Guys!" he hissed. "The column next to me has some kind of drawer in it. You'll have to lean in to me to see it."

Sailor was beside him, her head down. "Got it! Placing her thumbs along the top part of the crack and her fingers on the bottom, she began to tug. "It's really stuck in there."

"Let me help," said Emmett, squatting.

They clawed at the stone, prying and pulling, grunting and groaning.

"It's no use," spit Sailor. "It won't budge."

"Giving it . . . one . . . more . . . try!" Emmett lost his grip and fell backward. "She's right. It's stuck."

The three of them looked at one another, then at the floor, where a sliver of sunlight was crossing the bird-fish mosaic. Cruz felt its warmth on his fingertips for about 30 seconds. The beam passed over his hand, then vanished.

"It's four thirty," whispered Emmett.

Was that it?

Nothing was happening. Cruz felt himself go limp. He dropped his head. What had he done wrong now? He was about to take his hands off the mosaic, about to give up, when he saw a white flash.

"Look!" cried Sailor.

Cruz lifted his head. The eye of the birsh! Sitting in the space between the third and fourth fingers of his left hand, the eye was glowing!

"It's gotta be some kind of sensor," whispered Emmett.

Cruz inched his index finger over the black tiles that rimmed the eye, then onto the white and finally the lit black pupil.

They waited. And waited. And waited.

Sailor sighed. "Maybe we're supposed to—"

Eeeee-rrrrk!

It was the earsplitting sound of stone grinding against stone. The drawer was opening! It was sliding out of the side of the curved column.

"Yes!" shouted Cruz.

Emmett and Sailor carefully eased the drawer out the rest of the way. There, inside the chamber, was a miniature aqua parchment envelope. Two heads turned to Cruz. His hands trembling, Cruz reached inside the drawer and took out the envelope. There was no writing on it. He slid his finger under the back flap. He tipped the envelope, and the tattered folds of an aqua paper slid into his palm. It had weight to it. There was something inside. Holding his breath, Cruz peeled back one fold, then another. Lifting the third fold, his breath caught as he saw the slice of black marble.

They had done it! They had found the third cipher.

As day turned to night in the ancient city of Petra, three tired, hungry, and very happy explorers sat on the cool stone floor of a 1,600-year-old church.

Nobody said a word. Nobody had to.

20

TROTTING UP the steps to the fourth deck of *Orion,* Cruz shoved his hands into his pockets. His fingers closed around the cipher: three pieces of black stone now firmly attached to one another by their jigsaw-puzzle-like knobs and curved indentations.

"Hey, Cruz!" Turning, Cruz waited for Zane Patrick to catch up. "So are we ever going to get the scoop about where you, Emmett, and Sailor went over the weekend?"

"I told you already." He tried to play it cool. "We went ashore with Captain Iskandar to talk to some kids who are thinking about applying to the Academy. We told them what it's like and stuff. No big deal. You'll probably get asked to do it, too." Cruz clamped his lips tight. Was he talking too much? He sounded like he was talking too much.

Zane lifted his chin, as if he wasn't quite sure if he believed him.

Cruz needed to change the subject. Now. "Your team must be excited about going to Egypt, though, huh?"

"Egypt?"

"Yeah, you won the maze challenge, so I figured—"

"Oh, so you haven't heard?"

"Heard what?"

"We're going to Turkey."

"*What?*"

"Turkey, you know, the country?"

"I know the country, Zane, what I meant was—"

"Dugan told us about your looting tile. Said Professor Luben thinks it could be some kind of lost tomb or city or some big archaeological find and that we ought to go explore it. So we took a team vote and Turkey won."

Cruz was stunned. "Dugan convinced *you* to go to *our* site. Dugan? Marsh?"

Zane gave him a smirk. "He's not such a bad guy, you know."

"I know," said Cruz. He still didn't know why Dugan might have to leave the Academy. He had tried asking him about it when they were alone in the explorers' passage, but Dugan had shrugged it off: "Forget it. I'm fine. It's nothing."

Cruz wasn't so sure.

Zane headed for the next flight of stairs. "You coming up to watch the Leonids?"

"Yeah, but I have something to do first."

Cruz knew he couldn't put it off any longer. They had been back from Petra for four days and the ship would be putting in at Istanbul in less than 48 hours. He was running out of time to make copies of the cipher. Since Professor Luben's lessons hadn't involved the explorers using their PANDA units, Cruz had no choice but to take matters into his own hands. He was on his way to the tech lab to ask Fanchon—beg, if necessary—to let him borrow a PANDA.

Orion's science tech lab was located in the forward compartment of the fourth deck. It was divided into a maze of cubicles, each containing a technological wonder in various stages of development. As Cruz entered, he kept his hands in his pockets. He knew better than to touch anything. Or talk to it.

"Fanchon?" In the greenish glow of the lab, Cruz went up on his toes to see over the cubicles. "Dr. Vanderwick?"

Inside a nearby cubicle, he saw two large glass globes, one on top of the other, connected in the middle with a tube in the shape of a figure eight and a pump. Inside the lower globe, three green marbles were bouncing around in what appeared to be water. Those marbles sure looked like—

"Cruz!" Fanchon was stalking toward him in her red flip-flops. She was wearing a purple apron over a white sparkly tee and pink jeans. The front of her apron read *Forget Princess, Be a Scientist*.

Cruz pointed to the beaker. "Are those . . . ?"

"Eyeballs? Yeah," she said matter-of-factly. "Part of our artificial intelligence line. What do ya think? Too green?"

"Um, no . . . really lifelike."

"Optics has proved to be more of a challenge than I anticipated," said Fanchon. "We're making better progress on our olfactory receptors, so if you ever lose your sense of smell, stop on by and I can give it back to you in a snap." She giggled. "Or a sniff."

"Good to know."

Fanchon tucked a stray curl under a white headscarf dotted with penguins. "What's up?"

"I . . . uh . . . was wondering if I could borrow a PANDA unit to . . . uh . . . analyze a cool fossil I found in Barcelona."

"Hmmm." She swished her mouth from side to side as if it were filled with mouthwash. "I'm not supposed to check them out without faculty approval, but I guess it would be okay to let you use it in here."

"H-here?" Cruz felt his skin go prickly. He had planned to take the device back to his cabin, where he could analyze the cipher away from security cameras and prying eyes.

Fanchon went along the wall of cabinets, stopping about halfway down the row. Bending, she unlocked a door, reached in, and took a PANDA device out of a box. "Come on. I'll set you up where you won't be disturbed." Cruz followed her to one of the back cubicles. It was empty. She set the unit on the desk. "Will you be okay?"

"I do have a question," said Cruz. "I know I can upload the analytics to my tablet, but if I find any DNA on the . . . uh, fossil . . . can I upload the holo results, too? You know, to watch later."

"Absolutely. Once your analysis is complete, hit stop. Select 'holo-video file,' then find your name and hit send and it'll upload everything to your tablet, including DNA recovery info, which will allow you to project the hologram anywhere, anytime."

"Great."

"Let me know if you have any more questions."

"Actually . . . uh . . . I do have one, but it doesn't have anything to do with the PANDA."

"Shoot."

Cruz glanced down at her flip-flops and asked a question he had been dying to ask since he'd first met the tech lab chief. "Isn't it kind of dangerous to wear those in here? What if you spill a chemical or something on your feet?"

Fanchon let out a tiny snort. Reaching into a cubicle, she grabbed a pair of lab gloves and goggles. She tossed them to Cruz. While he put them on, she opened a nearby cabinet. Fanchon brought out a beaker of a ruby red liquid and held it out to him.

"What is it?"

"A combination of jalapeño pepper extract, fire ant venom, and a few other spicy chemicals." She held out her foot. "Pour it on my toes."

"Are you kidding?"

"Trust me. It'll be okay."

Cruz was defiant. "Nope. Nuh-uh. No way."

"Oh, great globs of goat cheese." She took the beaker and, as he watched in horror, tipped it. The bright red liquid streamed out, but instead of hitting her toes, it rolled off her foot, as if she were wearing a glass boot.

Cruz's jaw fell. "How did you—"

"Force field." She winked. "And that's all I'm saying. Any more questions?"

He rapidly shook his head.

Fanchon reached for a container that read *Chemical Spill Kit*. She took a cloth from the kit, patted the floor to absorb the liquid, placed the cloth in a plastic bag, and sealed it. "If you need me, I'll be on the other side of the lab in the cubicle with the micro food supplements. It's the one right behind the dinosaur eggs."

"Okay." Reaching for the PANDA, Cruz's head snapped around. Dinosaur eggs?

Too late to ask about it; the *splick-splack* sound of her flip-flops was fading away.

Cruz took the cipher from his pocket and held it in his cupped hand. He didn't want a security camera to get a look at it. Hunching over, he turned on the PANDA unit and pressed the blue ID button. When the screen read SCAN NOW, he slowly swept it across all three pieces of stone. A minute later, the results came up:

Item: non-foliated metamorphic limestone
Composition: calcium carbonate (CaCO$_3$),
quartz (SiO$_2$), graphite (C),
pyrite (FeS$_2$)
Common Name: black marble
Origin: Mexico
Age: 729 million years old

Cruz's finger hovered over the yellow button, the one that checked for DNA. His heart jumped. His mom's DNA could still be on the cipher. He didn't know why that scared him, but it did. It wouldn't mean anything if it was. It wouldn't change anything. So why was he so nervous to find out the truth? Cruz hesitated, then forced himself to push the yellow button. He waited for the "go" signal and slid the unit across the marble stones one more time. He heard a soft tone.

It was there! The unit had found DNA on the cipher.

What was he getting so excited about? Of course it had. Cruz had handled the stones. So had Lani, Sailor, Emmett, and Aunt Marisol. The device had probably identified all of their DNA. But what if there was more? Cruz knew he had 15 seconds before the unit began producing images of the life-forms the DNA belonged to. Actually, he was probably down to five seconds now. Four . . . three . . . two . . .

Cruz punched STOP.

If his mom's DNA was on the stone, he wanted to know. He wanted to see her. But not here. Along with the security cameras, Fanchon, and Sidril, who knows who else might be lurking nearby? Cruz uploaded the PANDA results to his tablet. He had just dropped the cipher back into his pocket when the tech lab chief popped around the corner. "Any trouble?"

"Nope." Cruz tapped the CLEAR button on the device, erasing all the data the PANDA unit had collected from his mom's cipher. He turned the unit off and handed it back to Fanchon. "Thanks."

"It's strange seeing you use this," she said, holding the unit in her palm as if it were a delicate flower. "Good strange, I mean. I used some of your mom's research into genome sequencing to develop the DNA scan program."

"You did?"

"Mmmm-hmmm. She was a brilliant geneticist. I think I've told you I've read everything she's ever written."

Cruz hadn't forgotten.

"I met her once, you know," said Fanchon.

"You . . . met my mom?"

"Well, I didn't meet her so much as hear her speak. She came to give a guest lecture at my college, sophomore year." Fanchon's eyes brightened. "She was incredible. She talked about advancements in genetics and said that as young scientists we had to keep asking questions and pushing boundaries because that's how you make the impossible possible. I confess I didn't quite understand what she meant at the time, but I think I do now."

Glancing around the lab, Cruz laughed. "Yes, you definitely push a lot of boundaries around here. Maybe someday I will, too."

"Someday?" She blew a raspberry. "How many other twelve-year-olds do you know who have talked to whales?"

He grinned. She had him there.

"Cliché to say this, I know, but your mom would have been proud of you."

Although he knew it was meant as a compliment, Cruz felt his stomach tighten. *Would* his mom be proud of him? He wasn't so sure. Is this what she would have done—made a copy of the cipher and given the real thing to the kidnappers? Or was there another way out of this mess, a better way that he hadn't thought of? Even though he was handing over her cipher to Nebula to save his dad, somehow it still felt like a betrayal. His mom had broken boundaries he had yet to see. She had stood up to Nebula, while he was giving in.

Cruz waited while Fanchon locked up the PANDA unit. The tech lab chief turned off the lights, and they left the lab. At the steps, Cruz started up as Fanchon headed down.

"Going up to see the Leonids?" she asked. When he nodded, she said, "Enjoy. Good night, Cruz."

"Good night, Fanchon." He trudged up one deck, his footsteps and his heart heavy.

Cruz could hear Professor Modi's soothing, singsong voice long before he entered the observatory. All the lights in the domed compartment were off, even those in the greenhouse. The explorers were clustered around their teacher, who was standing next to the door leading to the outer deck. "The Leonid meteor shower occurs every year in November, when Earth's orbit crosses through the trail of Comet Tempel-Tuttle..." he was saying.

In the darkness, Cruz found Emmett and Sailor.

"How'd it go?" whispered Emmett.

Cruz gave him a thumbs-up.

"The Leonids have produced some of the most intense meteor storms Earth has ever seen," said Professor Modi. "At peak times, the meteors will fall at a thousand an hour or more. About every thirty-three years, there is a major storm with tens of thousands of meteors per hour. We're in luck. This is a peak year, so we should see—"

"There's one!" called Bryndis, pointing up.

"And another!" yelled Tao.

They watched a pair of bluish white streaks of light rocket across a starry sky.

Zipping up his jacket, Dr. Modi opened the door. Cruz felt a blast of cool wind. All the explorers filed onto the aft deck. No one stayed in. Cruz went, too, though he didn't have his heavy coat.

Bryndis came to stand beside him at the rail. "Where's your jacket?"

He shrugged. "Forgot it?"

"You should go back inside. You can still see plenty of meteors from the dome."

"I'm fine," he said, trying to keep his mouth shut so she wouldn't see his teeth chattering.

"Come here." She flung her hood down. "You can share mine."

They each slipped an arm into a sleeve and held the jacket closed in front of them. As *Orion* sailed through the waters of the Mediterranean toward Greece, everyone tipped their heads back to watch for meteors.

"Some people believe comets bring bad luck," Bryndis whispered in his ear.

"Not me," he said, gazing up.

"Me either," she answered.

Suddenly, a shower of sparks filled the sky, followed by a chorus of "oooohs" from the explorers.

"Good thing we're not superstitious," said Bryndis. "Because if we were, that's a lifetime of bad luck."

A chill shook Cruz's spine. And it had nothing to do with the weather.

21

ROMANIA • CRIMEA • RUSSIA

BULGARIA • Black Sea • GEORGIA • ARMENIA

TURKEY • IRAN

ISTANBUL, TURKEY

NORTHERN CYPRUS • SYRIA • IRAQ
CYPRUS • LEBANON
Mediterranean Sea

▶ IT WAS Saturday, November 14.

Cruz had to be at the spice market in less than an hour.

Standing on the veranda outside his cabin, he took a deep breath to calm himself. The cool morning air smelled of both fish and coffee—not a good combination. *Orion* had put in at port in Istanbul sometime overnight, and Cruz was just now getting his first look at the most populous city in Turkey. From the harbor to the horizon, the gently sloping hills were blanketed with buildings. Ancient stone and modern glass-and-steel structures were packed together like mismatched furniture in an attic. Rising from the jumbled skyline, he saw the grand domes of centuries-old mosques and their decorative minarets, the tall spires from which Muslims are called to prayer. *Orion* was docked at a long terminal along the Eminönü estuary jetty, sandwiched between brightly painted tour boats with bubbled gold roofs. It was a few minutes after eight o'clock, but the walkway at the head of the pier was already crowded.

The veranda door opened. Emmett leaned out. "Ready for breakfast?"

Cruz shook his head. He could barely inhale, let alone eat.

According to his GPS, the spice bazaar was a 10-minute walk from the docks. Cruz just wanted this whole thing to be finished. Over. Done. Go to the market, wait for Nebula to contact him, hand over the cipher, and cross his fingers that his father would be released.

Emmett was motioning for Cruz to come inside. When he did, his roommate handed him a small piece of rubber no bigger than a pencil eraser.

"What's this?" asked Cruz.

"Earbud. It'll allow me to communicate with you while you're in the market without Nebula knowing. Also, I've patched into the signal from your comm pin so you can talk to me, too, without having to press the pin. This way, we'll be in constant contact."

"I don't know, Emmett." Cruz let the bud roll across his palm. "They said to come alone—"

"And you *will* be. But, Cruz, you can't go in there blind. What if something happens? What if they grab you? What if they don't show? We *have* to stay in touch."

Cruz bit his lip. Emmett had a point. And the earbud *was* small. Nebula would never see it. "All right, but just the two of us. Nobody else."

"Nobody else."

His tablet was chiming. Cruz's breath caught. He had a message and he was pretty sure he knew who it was from.

Today. 9 a.m.
The Spice Bazaar
Stall 19, Galata Sweets
Try the Turkish delight!
Once we have the three sections of the cipher,
your father will be released.
Come alone.

"Three pieces!" groaned Cruz. "They know I have three pieces of the cipher."

Emmett shook his head. "Why am I not surprised? They seem to have eyes and ears everywhere."

Cruz reached for his uniform jacket. He'd recalled Mell from her post outside the mystery door on B deck, and she was now safely tucked inside his upper-right pocket. His octopod was in his lower-right front pocket, where he could get to it quickly, if necessary. The full cipher was in his lower-left front pocket. Emmett and Cruz had made their copy of the pieces yesterday on their 3D printer. They were now back in Hubbard's life vest.

Cruz fitted the bud in his right ear.

Emmett slipped on his headset. "Can you hear me?"

His voice boomed in Cruz's head. "Ow!" Cruz threw a hand to his ear.

Flying to his computer, Emmett tapped a few keys. "Sorry. Okay now?"

Cruz's head was still ringing. "Yeah."

Emmett took a seat at his desk. "Talk to me."

"Cruz Coronado to Emmett Lu. Testing, testing."

"We're set. All systems go," said Emmett, holding out his fist.

Cruz bumped it. "Where's Sailor? I've got to get going."

"I'm sure she'll be here. I'll find her."

Cruz slid his GPS sunglasses up on his head, tucked his tablet under his arm, and started for the door.

"Be careful," said Emmett. "Don't do anything crazy."

"That's the plan," muttered Cruz.

Shutting the cabin door, he headed down the explorers' passage and through the atrium. Aunt Marisol had arranged things with Taryn so he could leave the ship on his own without getting into trouble. Trotting down the gangway to the pier, Cruz's legs felt like two sticks of licorice. He told himself it was from being at sea. It was the best lie he could think of. He slid his sunglasses down and followed the route to the market his GPS mapped out for him. Cruz crossed a parking lot, then a wide, heavily traveled highway called Ragıp Gümüşpala. The spice market was located in a big L-shaped building next to a beautiful 17th-century mosque that Cruz's GPS identified as Yeni Cami, or New Mosque. Cruz headed across the square toward the arched stone entrance to the market.

"Stall 19, Galata Sweets," he whispered to himself, then with a deep breath, *"Fortes fortuna adiuvat."*

"Fortune favors the brave," a voice in his ear translated Dr. Hightower's favorite saying.

Cruz jumped. "I forgot you were listening, Emmett. I'm here. I'm at the market."

"I know. I'm tracking you via your GPS equipment."

Naturally.

"İyi şanslar," said Emmett.

"Huh?"

"It's Turkish for 'good luck.'"

"Thanks," said Cruz, joining the flow of shoppers heading into the market.

The bazaar was an explosion for the senses. Jostling his way down an aisle with more shoppers than space, Cruz was overwhelmed by the vivid colors, exotic smells, and sheer volume of goods. Every space in every little store was filled to its arched rafters with items—scarves, pillows, vases, jewelry, plates, tapestries, rugs, lamps, and wind chimes. Food was everywhere. Bakery cases brimmed with baklava, jellied candies, and chocolate. Cruz passed tall jars filled with dried apricots, figs, mulberries, and pineapple rings, and still more jars packed with pistachios, hazelnuts, almonds, and walnuts. Oils in every color of the rainbow glittered in crystal bottles. Strings of chopped and dried peppers, eggplants, and okra swung from hooks. Barrels overflowed with teas: mint, hibiscus, apple, jasmine, relaxation—there was even one called love tea. And the spices! Shoppers scooped spices from open bins containing perfect pyramids of bright red paprika, yellow curry,

golden cumin, white ginger, and burgundy sumac.

The shops had signs hanging above them with their name and stall number. Some were in neon and easy to find. Cruz kept moving through the bazaar, spotting the numbers and working his way into the teens. He turned sideways to squeeze through a choke point in the crowd. Looking behind him, Cruz caught a glimpse of reddish blond hair sticking out of a black headscarf. "Uh-oh."

"What's wrong?" asked Emmett.

"I'm being followed."

"The man in the cowboy boots?"

"I'm pretty sure it's Officer Dover."

"Ship security?" Emmett's voice went up a full octave.

"Yep."

"Aunt Marisol," they said in unison.

"She's wearing a head covering, so maybe they won't notice her," mumbled Cruz.

"Hopefully, she'll keep a safe distance," said Emmett.

Above the crowd, Cruz saw a vertical red neon sign: GALATA SWEETS, 19. His pulse quickened. "I'm almost there." He shoved both hands into his pockets, the right latching on to the octopod, the left, the cipher. "Mell, on," he said. Just in case.

Cruz turned into the store. It couldn't have been more than 20 feet long and half as wide but, like all the other shops, it was packed floor to ceiling with candies, nuts, dried fruits, and teas. Cruz slowly made his way around the store to the back counter, where he pretended to be interested in a case of speckled candy-coated chocolate balls that were so big that at first he thought they were eggs. Thank goodness the signs were in English!

A plump Turkish woman who could have been his grandmother peered at him between the jars of candy. "*Merhaba.*"

"Hello," said Cruz's universal translator.

"*Merhaba,*" said Cruz.

The old woman toddled out. She was carrying a small tray with several dark red squares with rounded edges. She grinned at him. *"Türk lokumu denemelisin."*

"You must try my Turkish delight," said his translator.

Cruz remembered Nebula's instructions. Releasing his octopod, he reached for a square of the red candy dusted with powdered sugar. The soft candy tasted sweet, a cross between strawberries and cherries. It held a crunchy surprise inside—pistachios. It *was* good.

The woman leaned in. "Leave the store and turn right," she said in English. "Walk straight until you see the man in the black-and-white-striped cap. Give him the cipher."

Cruz hurried out of the shop. Swinging right, his eyes swept the path in front of him. He glanced back. "I don't see Officer Dover."

"Don't worry about her," said Emmett. "Look for the man in the striped cap."

"I'm looking, I'm looking."

If only the market weren't so busy. Cruz kept moving, his eyes darting left and right, in case the man came out of a store.

"Cruz?" It was Emmett. "Lani's on the phone."

"Not a good time," hissed Cruz.

"She's with your aunt and ... the clue ... observe ..."

"What?" snapped Cruz. "Emmett, you're cutting out. Repeat."

There! Ahead, a stocky man in a black-and-white-striped cap and a black peacoat was heading Cruz's way.

"I think I see him." Cruz's hand tightened around the cipher in his pocket. To be sure he had the right guy, he went to the far right of the aisle. The man mirrored his movements. "It's Nebula, all right," said Cruz. "I'm about fifty feet from him."

"Cruz ... did you ... okay?" Emmett was still cutting out.

As their gap closed, Cruz's heart beat faster. He felt light-headed. His hands were cold, his feet hot. They were now a mere 20 feet apart. Cruz brought a frozen hand with the cipher from his pocket. He held his left arm out and turned his fist down. The man's head was lowered, so Cruz couldn't see his face. A black glove went out, palm up. In a matter of seconds, they would pass each other. Cruz began to uncurl his fingers. He felt the marble stones slide between them ...

"Abort!" Emmett's voice ricocheted through his head.

"What?"

"Abort, abort! Cruz, don't give him the cipher!" shouted Emmett. *"Do not give him the cipher."*

Cruz clamped his fist closed, catching the cipher a second before it would have dropped into the outstretched glove.

"What the ... Hey, you!"

Cruz had no intention of turning around. He began to run, his heart pumping wildly. Cruz hoped his roommate knew what he was talking about, because if he didn't, Cruz had just cost his father his life. "Emmett," he huffed, slowing to a jog. "What's going on?"

"Your dad is free ... he's all right. Do you hear me? I said *your dad's all right.* Lani and your aunt rescued him ... police have the kidnappers."

A glove clamped on to Cruz's wrist. "I want that cipher, kid."

"No!" Cruz tried to pull away, but the man in the cap was too strong. He began to bend Cruz's arm back, pushing him to the ground. Pain shot through Cruz's wrist. His knees buckled. Cruz tried to keep his fingers locked, but his opponent was peeling them back, one by one. Desperate, Cruz threw his other hand up onto the man's glove to keep him from ripping away the cipher.

His octopod! One spritz from the blue-ringed orb would get this guy to back off, but to reach the weapon in his pocket, Cruz would have to let go with his right hand. His attacker would easily pry apart the rest of his fingers and take the cipher. The octopod wasn't going to work. Cruz had only one option left.

"Mell, defense mode," he said between gritted teeth. "Target—"

A hand was over his mouth. Someone else was behind him. Another attacker! Cruz couldn't finish giving Mell directions. Cruz was on his knees now, hanging on to the cipher with only his ring and pinkie fingers. He couldn't hold on much longer ...

Cruz heard a cry in front of him. Then another yelp from behind.

A yellow cloud descended on him. The death grip on his hand was suddenly gone. His mouth was free, too, however, his eyes and nose were starting to burn.

Someone was yanking him up. A hand latched on to his. "*Run!*"

Half blind, his throat on fire, Cruz stumbled through the crowded market. He clung to his rescuer with one hand and the cipher with the other. Tears streamed down his face, transforming the colorful bazaar into an oil painting left out in the rain. Was that a black headscarf bobbing in front of him? It was! Officer Dover! She wove through the jammed aisle with Cruz in tow, expertly dodging strollers and shopping bags. Officer Dover didn't slow up until they were through the front of the market and halfway across the main square.

"Stop ... please ..." His lungs heaving, Cruz couldn't take another step.

She flung the headscarf aside. "I think we're safe now."

Cruz nearly collapsed. "Sailor?"

"Sailor!" Emmett was still in his head.

"We thought you were Officer Dover!" cried Cruz, still trying to wipe the sting from his eyes.

"Hardly. You gave her the slip five minutes ago."

"I was supposed to come alone."

"Yeah, well ... what kind of friend would I be if I let you do that?"

Standing in the middle of the square, a blur of people crisscrossing around him, it hit Cruz. He'd been wrong. His vision blurry, he looked up at his friend, struggling to rewrap her headscarf. Sailor. Lani. Emmett. Taryn. Fanchon. Cruz may not have had his family to turn to these past few weeks, but he wasn't alone.

Never had been.

22

▶**THORNE PRESCOTT** *hung*
an elbow out the window of his truck as it rumbled up the side of
the volcano. The road to the top of Mauna Kea curved back and
forth between bare brown hills for 18 miles, slowly rising to an
elevation of almost 14,000 feet.

A few miles from the summit, Prescott couldn't contain his grin.
Genius. That's what it was. Who would ever guess that within one
of the many domed observatories perched on the highest point
in Hawaii there would be anything—or anyone—other than tele-
scopes and research equipment?

But there was.

Prescott glanced at his phone on the seat beside him. It
wouldn't be long now. Soon, Swan would call to confirm that
Nebula had the cipher and the team could be on their way.
They would have to leave Marco behind, of course, in the hidden
soundproof room beneath Gemini Observatory. Prescott was
sorry about that, but it was business. Marco had been kept alive
this long only in the event that Cruz had demanded to talk to his
father before surrendering the cipher. Once Nebula had it, well . . .

Business.

Rounding the last bend, Prescott saw flashing red and blue
lights. His heart fluttered. He told himself not to panic. Another
observatory was in the way, so he couldn't be sure . . . there could
be something else going on . . .

Right?

Gripping the steering wheel with white knuckles, Prescott
veered off the access road into the looped driveway leading to

Gemini. It was his worst fear. A half dozen police cars surrounded the silver dome. Officers were swarming the place.

Prescott frantically rolled up his window. Slumping down, he slowed to pass the scene. Scorpion was being taken out of the building in handcuffs. He didn't see Komodo. Marco was standing outside the main door, a blanket over his shoulders. Marisol Coronado stood next to him. A teenage girl was there, too, but Prescott had never seen her before. As his truck went by, the girl looked right at him. He turned to look forward. Prescott was on a circular road. He had no choice but to continue around another smaller observatory and go past Gemini again to get back to the main road. The second time he went by the scene, Prescott saw Scorpion in the back of a police car. The girl was still staring his way. Although the wind whipped her chin-length chocolate hair around her face, Prescott could see her eyes.

She was angry. No, furious.

Cruz didn't have any siblings. So who was she?

Prescott drove down the mountain, his eyes darting to his rearview mirror looking for flashing lights every other second. Did Nebula have the cipher? Or had that part of the plan fallen apart, too? He would have to make contact with Zebra and Jaguar to see how things stood on the other end, but Prescott had a gut feeling the news wasn't going to be good. One thing was for sure: Brume would not be happy they had failed. Again.

Time was running out.

Prescott let up on the brake, coasting faster down the hill. He would be glad to leave paradise.

The sooner the better.

23

▶ **IT WAS** the best early birthday present he could have hoped for, seeing his dad, Aunt Marisol, and Lani all happily crammed together in front of the camera. They were waving at him from the Goofy Foot.

Cruz waved back. "I can't believe you rescued Dad."

Aunt Marisol and Lani beamed.

"I gotta know," said Sailor, leaning in. "How did you figure out Nebula had taken Mr. Coronado from the sugar mill to Mauna Kea?"

Cruz's aunt looked to Lani. "You want to take that one?"

"It took a while." Lani tucked a lock of hair behind her ear. "I knew Mr. C had left us the silverware tied up with the necklace for a reason, but I couldn't put the pieces together, or should I say the *Pisces* together."

Everyone groaned.

Listening to his best friend, Cruz did not take his eyes off his father. Standing behind Lani, in a bright red-and-orange floral shirt, his dad was grinning, but his face was gaunt, his eyes puffy.

"Then it dawned on me," continued Lani. "Cruz, I remembered last year, your dad took us up to Mauna Kea for that habitat restoration project for school. We spent the whole day on the volcano replanting native *silversword* plants. Get it? Silversword—*silverware*? Still, I wasn't completely sure that's what it meant, and even if I was right, I still had no idea where on Mauna Kea they could have taken him. So I looked up all the observatories, weather stations, and research facilities in the area, and I came across Gemini Observatory. It's the only one named after a constellation, just the way your mom's Pisces necklace is a constellation. It clicked. I thought maybe your dad wrapped the necklace around the silverware to tell us, in the best way he could, that he was being taken to the Gemini Observatory on Mauna Kea."

Cruz's dad patted Lani's shoulder.

Lani tipped her head. "So I told your aunt—"

"Honestly, it seemed a bit of a stretch to me." Aunt Marisol picked up the story, "But we had no other leads or ideas about what the clue could mean, and you know how persuasive Lani can be."

Cruz grunted. Boy, did he.

"I told Lani we couldn't go alone," said his aunt, "so she *persuaded* one of the detectives to come with us. At first, everything at the observatory looked normal and I was sure we were on the wrong track. There was a scientist from the university on duty, but he checked out okay. He even showed us around the inside of the building."

"I knew something wasn't right," interjected Lani. "I just knew it."

Aunt Marisol made a face. "She wouldn't let us leave. Since we'd gone all that way, the detective agreed to a *short* stakeout. We drove down to the parking lot of one of the other observatories, waited, and watched. About forty-five minutes later, we got lucky. A man went to the back of the building and opened a door to some kind of underground bunker we hadn't even noticed was there. When the officer saw that the man was armed, he called for backup and—"

"We got 'em!" cried Lani. "Well, we got two out of three."

"They'll get him," said Cruz's dad. "They'll get Cobra or Tom or whatever his name really is."

Cruz had a funny feeling that Cobra or Tom or whatever-his-name-really-is also owned a pair of snakeskin-print cowboy boots.

"We'd better go," said his dad. "It's getting late for you, and I have a lot of work to catch up on."

"I have a ship to get back to," said Aunt Marisol.

"I have a ton of homework," groaned Lani.

Everyone chuckled.

They said their goodbyes, and Cruz left his cabin with Sailor. They had about a half hour until lights-out, but he needed to burn off some energy. Maybe he would head up to the lounge to see if anyone was playing a game. Or go to the observatory to watch the Leonids. And to think. Cruz still had more than a few questions to ponder—questions like: Who was the English girl in red who had saved him at Petra? Where was Malcolm Rook and what did he want? And why was Jericho Miles and at least one other Synthesis scientist hiding in the belly of the ship?

Up ahead, Taryn's door opened. Hubbard trotted out, his green ball in his mouth. When he saw Cruz, the Westie dropped the ball and bounded toward him. Cruz knelt and patted his knee. Hubbard ran down the passage at full throttle, tail up, ears flapping. He jumped into Cruz's arms, licking, licking, licking with his wet pink tongue.

His face glazed with dog drool, Cruz could only laugh. How could he have forgotten to include Hubbard among those who had been there for him? After all, the little Westie had given Cruz the best gift of all.

Love.

24

ROMANIA CRIMEA RUSSIA
BULGARIA Black Sea GEORGIA
KONYA, TURKEY ARMENIA
TURKEY IRAN
NORTHERN CYPRUS SYRIA IRAQ
CYPRUS LEBANON
Mediterranean Sea

DIG, SCOOP, DROP.

Dig, scoop, drop.

Cruz had gotten into an easy rhythm. Gently pierce the ground with the small shovel, scoop up a chunk of dirt, and toss it into the hover sifter. Once Cruz had put 10 or so shovelfuls of dirt into the sifter, a wood-framed box with a screen for a bottom suspended in midair, the solar-powered device would slowly shake the contents from side to side. The dirt then fell through the mesh to a square bucket below, leaving any artifacts behind in the sifter. Cruz had been digging, scooping, and dropping all morning and had only found a couple of bone fragments, a shard of 18th-century pottery, and a one-lira coin from 1947. Not exactly earth-shattering discoveries.

Cruz didn't care. Archaeology was fun. It was not, however, easy. Or speedy.

Twenty-three explorers had been eager and enthusiastic when the Academy's plane had whisked them from Istanbul to Konya, in central Turkey. With the snowcapped twin peaks of Mount Hasan in the distance, they had trekked a few hours to the rolling brown plains outside of Aksaray. The city was once an important stop along the Silk Road, the ancient trade route connecting the Far East to western Europe. Professor Luben and Aunt Marisol had led them to the area where Team Cousteau had spotted the ruins on their looting tile. Then it was time to search for the circles that had appeared on their satellite map. Six days later, they were still at it—digging, sifting, scraping, and brushing—with little to show for their efforts but a broken two-foot section of a curved wall. Their PANDA units revealed the stone wall was once part of a temple in a Neolithic city more than 9,000 years ago!

That was exciting enough for Cruz. He was thrilled that Team Cousteau had discovered a lost city. It didn't matter that the work went slowly or that they weren't finding much. He was outdoors in a valley under a big ice blue sky with white puffs of train-engine clouds gliding past with his friends and Aunt Marisol, even if she was a bit too busy to dig alongside him.

Cruz nudged Dugan, who was working next to him. "I meant to thank you for convincing Team Magellan to come here. I don't know how you did it, but thanks."

Sailor, Emmett, and Bryndis chimed in. "Yeah, thanks, Dugan."

Dugan lifted a shoulder. "No big deal." But the grin on his face said it *was* a big deal.

As Cruz dropped more dirt into the sifter, his aunt scurried past. "Tao, the idea is to gently scrape with the trowel, not stab the ground. You don't want to damage anything under the surface." She bent, took Tao's hand, and readjusted her wrist. "Relax your grip a little. There you go."

"Professor Coronado, how long does a dig take?" asked Felipe.

"Depends," answered Aunt Marisol. "It's like a treasure hunt. You could find something amazing in your very next shovelful, or a major discovery could take months—even years."

"Years?" Felipe's mouth dropped.

"In A.D. 79, the entire Italian city of Pompeii was buried by an eruption from Mount Vesuvius," explained Cruz's aunt. "It took several centuries for archaeologists to excavate such a large site. They didn't finish until the early twenty-first century."

"And we're *still* finding secret chambers in the pyramids at Giza," boomed Professor Luben, galloping down the slope behind them. He was wearing khakis, a tan shirt, and a matching safari vest covered in a million tiny pockets. "You can't rush exploration, and I, for one, wouldn't want to. The adventure that leads to the discovery is half the fun. Okay, it's most of the fun. Nope, I gotta say it, it's *all* the fun."

Cruz and his teammates laughed.

"Keep at it, explorers," said Professor Luben. "Somewhere, something unknown is waiting to be known."

Felipe glanced at his feet and sighed as if to say, "I doubt I'm standing on it."

Aunt Marisol turned to Cruz. "You're not upset that we'll be spending your birthday here, are you?"

Cruz's birthday was tomorrow.

"No! This is a pretty cool present."

"Good." She sighed. "Because I was so hoping you'd like archaeology fieldwork, even though I know it can be tedious at times—What in the world is Zane doing?"

Cruz squinted. A few yards off, Zane was pounding the ground with the blunt end of his square shovel.

Aunt Marisol ran toward him. "Zane, careful there, we're not chopping wood..."

Cruz went back to work.

Dig, scoop, drop.

Dig, scoop, drop.

"Speaking of adventure," came the whisper in his ear. Cruz turned to look up at Professor Luben, who was also looking up. "Interesting outcrop, don't you think?"

Was it? Cruz followed his gaze up to the craggy gray rock at the top of the hill.

"It's the only rock shelter around for miles." With a wink, his teacher picked a shovel off the pile, spun it to lay it against his shoulder, and headed across the field toward Team Earhart.

Cruz kept staring up at the slope. He knew what Professor Luben was getting at. A natural shelter would be a good place for people to take refuge—ancient people. It could be fun to explore. Cruz looked at the hole at his feet. He sure wasn't having much luck here. He'd take a quick break and be back before anyone knew he was gone.

Adding a PANDA unit and a small trowel to his backpack, Cruz headed up the slope. As he hiked, the terrain became rockier. It took him a few tries to find a path between the tightly packed boulders. The hollow outcrop at the top of the hill wasn't large, maybe 15 feet deep by 25 feet long by 5 feet high. The branches of overgrown bushes brushed the top of his head as he slipped under the flat rock of the roof. The opening of the shelter faced north, and since it was late afternoon, it was pretty dark inside. Tapping the shadow badge on his uniform, Cruz closed his eyes. He pictured a bioluminescent jellyfish pulsing through the ocean. When he opened his eyes again, his uniform was glowing. Yep. Better than any flashlight! And it was all thanks to Lumagine, Emmett's mind-control fabric, and Fanchon's skill at adapting the technology to their uniforms.

It smelled like wet, warm dirt. Cruz crept to the back wall of the cave. He ran his hands along the cold, nubby surface. Cruz saw a pair of horizontal, dark red squiggles. Beside them was a crude stick figure drawn in the same red ocher. An ancient cave painting! They had just been reading about parietal art in anthropology class, too. Professor Luben and Aunt Marisol would love this! Cruz kept inching along, carefully following the massive stone wall from one corner to the other. Then he saw the handprint. They had learned about these types of prints in class. It looked to be a stenciled silhouette; that's where a hand was placed on the wall and pigment was either dabbed along the edges or blown through a tube around the fingers, leaving behind a silhouette on the rock. Cruz wondered how old it was. Five thousand years? Ten? His PANDA unit would tell him.

But first...

Cruz couldn't resist putting his palm on the ancient handprint. It was almost a perfect match. He was about to reach into his backpack for the PANDA when he felt a tremor. The rock was moving! It slid backward a few feet, then stopped. A space had opened up. The crevice was barely big enough for Cruz to squish a shoulder into. However, before he did, Cruz planted his feet. He didn't want the dirt under him giving way. With his feet solid, his hands clamped firmly on to the cave wall, he leaned in. Cruz tipped his chin down. He saw only darkness.

"Hello?" he called.

His voice echoed back to him. "Helloooooooo?"

A secret chamber! Cool! Cruz would have to get a photo before he headed back to tell—

He felt a jolt, and suddenly, Cruz was falling . . .

Skin was scraping rock.

Falling . . .

A point punctured his spine.

Falling . . .

End over end over end over end over end.

Cruz hit the unforgiving ground with a bone-crunching thud. Pain shot through his shoulder. All the air knocked from his chest, he gasped for life. Cruz took several minutes to catch his breath. With a groan, he rolled up on his side, and came face-to-face with a skull.

"Argggggh!" he cried, scooting backward until his spine smashed into stone.

Heart thumping, lungs wheezing, Cruz wrapped his arms around his knees and pulled them into his chest. "Okay, don't panic . . . Get a grip, Cruz."

By the glow of his uniform, Cruz saw that he was at the bottom of a stone cavern. Alone. Well, not completely alone. There was the skull. And, as he looked around, dozens more.

He tipped his head back. He could not see daylight. Using the wall for balance, Cruz got to his feet. His body felt battered and beaten, as if he'd wiped out on the biggest, ugliest wave ever. Cruz limped around the perimeter of the wall, feeling for an opening, inlet, or tunnel that might lead out of this place.

Nothing.

Cruz touched his shoulder. His pack was gone! He searched the ground. It wasn't there. It must have gotten snagged on a rock on the way down.

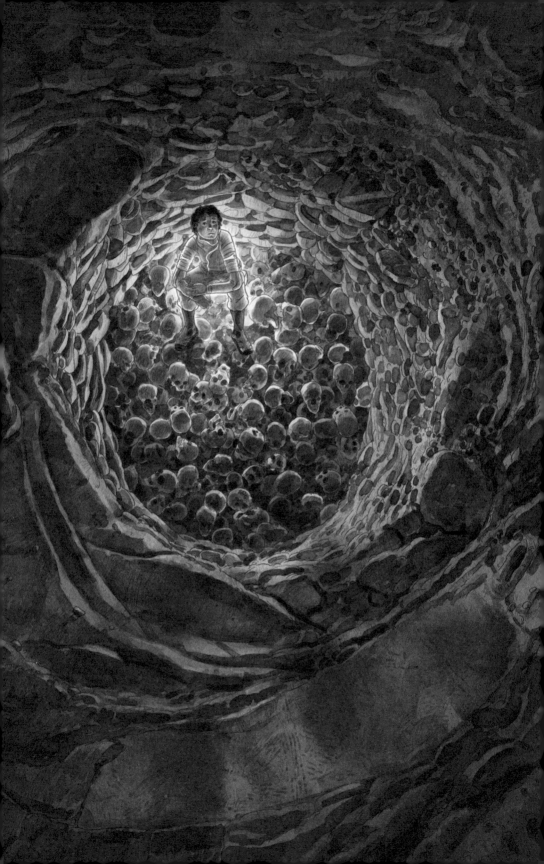

Or maybe he had left it at the surface. He couldn't remember. His phone and tablet were inside, so he couldn't make a call out. Mell couldn't help him, either. She was back on *Orion* getting a software upgrade. Cruz tapped his comm pin. "Cruz Coronado to Marisol Coronado."

No response.

"Cruz Coronado to Emmett Lu."

Again, nothing.

He tried every explorer, then Fanchon and Taryn, but it was no use. He had a feeling the signal wasn't getting out.

Cruz could hear water dripping. His shoulder throbbed. His head, too.

He sagged against the wall. There was nothing to do now but wait for help to arrive. If it ever did. Cruz drifted off into a fitful sleep. He had a dream that someone pushed him and he was falling and falling and falling ...

Cruz woke up with a start. For one brief minute he thought he had dreamed everything, but he soon realized he was still at the bottom of the cavern. The cool dampness sent a chill through him. His stomach gurgled. His head felt foggy. His OS band indicated he had a concussion, along with a bruised shoulder, a broken right big toe, and a fever of 100.1. The glow from his bioluminescent uniform was beginning to fade. How long had he been here anyway?

Cruz glanced at his OS band. It read *11/29, 12:09 a.m.*

Eight hours.

Were they looking for him? Would they even know where to look?

November 29. His birthday. Some present, huh?

Cruz let out a tortured laugh. "Ha-ha!"

It echoed back, taunting him. "Ha-haaaaa!"

Stuck at the bottom of a shaft certainly wasn't how Cruz had expected to spend his birthday. But he was alive. That was something worth celebrating, wasn't it? Nebula had vowed to get rid of him before he turned 13. They had failed. Cruz looked around his dark prison of stone.

Or had they?

THE TRUTH BEHIND THE FICTION

Explorers and archaeologists are history detectives, using clues left behind from ancient animals or civilizations to determine what our world was like thousands or even millions of years ago. Over time they have uncovered ruins of buildings, shards of pottery, fragments of bone, and fossils of extinct animals using simple tools and even their bare hands. Recent developments in technology have led to supercool advancements in archaeological research to allow finding often hidden or hard-to-reach spaces just waiting to be explored. What secrets are waiting to be uncovered? Check out these National Geographic explorers on the forefront of discovery.

BETH SHAPIRO

Evolutionary biologist Beth Shapiro may not have a fictional PANDA unit at her fingertips to be able to identify the origin, type, and age of human remains, fossils, and artifacts, but studying DNA has given her a remarkable window into the past. By retrieving DNA from ancient plants and animals, Shapiro is able to trace changes in diversity and populations over time. Science has typically explained the mass extinction of mammoths, mastodons, and saber-toothed cats 10,000 years ago as due to human overhunting or major changes in climate and vegetation. However, new studies of ancient DNA have shown that the true beginning of this huge extinction dates back tens of thousands of years to before the arrival of humans or the peak of the last ice age. The PANDA unit featured in *The Double Helix* was inspired by Shapiro's research. Imagine a world where you can scan any artifact for ancient DNA and pull up a realistic hologram of the source it came from!

SARAH PARCAK

How can satellites in outer space help us sleuth for civilizations far beneath Earth's soil? As real-life pioneering space archaeologist Sarah Parcak could tell you, archaeologists can search for unknown sites all around the world by using high-tech images from space satellites. Experts can pinpoint potential dig locations that are covered by cities, forests, or layers of soil, bringing to the surface everything from pyramids to temples, from homes to entire cities, all from the comfort of their computer desk. While the human eye can only see light on the visible spectrum, satellites use different kinds of sensors to see infrared light, UV light, and microwaves. Microwaves are what allow scientists to see objects underground. This ground-breaking technology is being utilized not only to uncover import-ant sites, but also to help combat looting. Cruz and his classmates examine several satellite maps and identify pits where someone may have stolen precious archaeological treasures. But you don't have to be a student at Explorer Academy or an expert space archaeologist like Parcak to help. Parcak created GlobalXplorer°, an online tool that allows volunteers to see space satellite images, look for looting holes, and potentially find more incredible discoveries of their own!

NORA SHAWKI

Dr. Luben asks the explorers to analyze an Egyptian coffin and tell him what they can discover about the person who rested inside. By investigating the symbols on the coffin, they realize that Shesepa-muntayesher was a lady of the house. Without the coffin, the students wouldn't be able to learn about her life. It's up to archaeologists like Nora Shawki to help bring such incredible relics back from the past. Shawki has helped to excavate on dig sites all over Egypt, focusing currently on the Nile Delta. Here, she uses geophysical surveying, essentially taking a giant x-ray scan of a location, in order to understand where and how to dig. She says the Nile Delta "won't exist in the next forty years," because so many people are encroaching on the area, making it all the more urgent to locate settlements now. She believes that archaeology isn't just about digging up golden sarcophagi and fancy jewelry of royals—it's about learning what everyday people's lives were like back in the day. "In history, anything is something," Shawki says. "It's like we are holding it between our hands, and we are the ones contributing to its interpretation."

MARINA ELLIOTT

When Cruz gets separated from his group, he winds up with some newfound company: dozens of skulls! For many people this would be a terrifying discovery, but for biological anthropologist Marina Elliott, finding and investigating human remains is the rush of a lifetime. In 2013, famed paleoanthropologist Lee Berger asked Elliott and five other female scientists to join him in excavating Rising Star, a cave in South Africa. The "Underground Astronauts," as they'd come to be nicknamed, had to venture through exceptionally tight passages, sometimes only eight inches wide, navigate through the dark, avoid a deadly ridge called Dragon's Back, and slide down a 39-foot chute before they came to the resting place of one of the most astonishing discoveries in recent years: *Homo naledi,* a new species of human relative. And with a massive archaeology find under her belt, Elliott believes that "it's just exciting to realize that the great age of exploration isn't over with—that there still are places to explore and there are things to find."

LEE BERGER

Lee Berger, lead paleoanthropologist of the team that discovered *Homo naledi,* has been digging into human origins in Africa for the past 30 years. The *Homo naledi* find was puzzling because of the mysterious way that the creatures appeared to be buried. There were no teeth marks on the bones to indicate that a predator dragged them deep into the cave. There were no other animal remains in the cave, so the entrance was probably sealed off. Moreover, some of the remains appeared to have had flesh on them when they were deposited in the cave. These clues suggested that the creatures were purposefully buried there. Scientists have long known that animals react to the death of their companions. Elephants, great apes, dolphins, horses, rabbits, cats, dogs, and some birds have all shown signs of grieving their lost loved ones. But ritual, purposeful burial is different, and was thought to be a humans-only activity. "We actually don't have the whole story of human evolution. These discoveries are telling us that there's a lot out there to be found," Berger says. And indeed, this revolutionary find makes us question what we thought we knew about evolution and rethink our connection to our animal ancestors.

To learn more about these topics and the passionate explorers who study them, check them out at the Explorer Academy website!

exploreracademy.com

EXPLORER ACADEMY

BOOK 4:
THE STAR DUNES

24.7681° S | 15.2959° E

Getting on all fours, Cruz began to crawl around the perimeter of the cave. There *had* to be a way out.

"Or not." He grimaced, gently rolling a skull out of his path.

Ten minutes later, Cruz was huffing and about to take a break, when he realized his shoes were wet. If water was getting in, it had to come from somewhere. This could be a way out!

The grotto was quickly beginning to fill. Cruz had to get to higher ground.

Fortunately, *Orion*'s science tech lab chief, Fanchon Quills, had designed their uniforms to be waterproof, but Cruz had a feeling Fanchon hadn't expected he would have to swim in the thing. In another few minutes, however, that's exactly what he was going to have to do.

Closing the collar of his uniform, Cruz felt something scrape the back of his neck. He reached behind him, his fingers closing around a metal tab. That's right! Every explorer's jacket was equipped with two critical survival items: a parachute, which wouldn't help him here, and a flotation device, which most definitely would! Except Cruz wasn't sure how to inflate the thing. He could almost hear his adviser, Taryn Secliff, say, *You'd know what to do if you hadn't glossed over the uniform instruction manual.*

"I know, Taryn, I know ..." Cruz yanked open his belt and unzipped his jacket. Wrestling free of the sleeves, he whipped the coat inside out. He found a small plastic tab near the collar. It was engraved with a *P*—for "parachute," no doubt. Okay, so where was the one to the float? Frantically, he went down the lining, searching for an *F* tab. He didn't find one. Cruz moaned. "How in the world am I supposed to activate this dumb flotation device?"

"Personal flotation device deployment confirmed." The calm female voice startled him. It was Fanchon!

"Cruz Coronado, please prepare for PFD deployment," said Fanchon. Her instructions were coming from his OS band! Smart. He should have known that when all else failed, he could count on his OS band for help.

**Read a longer excerpt from *The Star Dunes*
at exploreracademy.com.**

ACKNOWLEDGMENTS

If you want to explore the world, read a book. If you want to explore yourself, write one. I've been extraordinarily fortunate to have some incredible people supporting my long journey of self-discovery: first and foremost, my parents, Dean and Shirley Strain, who saw that spark in me when I wrote my first ghost story as a kid and stoked the fire; my husband, Bill, who's read every book I've ever written (even the ones about middle school girl power); my sister of the heart, Debbie Thoma, who has known me forever and loves me anyway; and my family, Jacques, Jennie, Lori Dru, Dean, Tammy, Austin, Trina, Bailey, and Carter. I am also lucky to have the most amazing team ever assembled in publishing: Becky Baines, Jennifer Rees, Jennifer Emmett, Erica Green, Eva Absher-Schantz, Scott Plumbe, Gareth Moore, Ruth Chamblee, Caitlin Holbrook, Holly Saunders, Ann Day, and so many others who helped breathe life into this project. This series would not have been possible without the real explorers of National Geographic. Thanks to Gemina Garland-Lewis, Nizar Ibrahim, Zoltan Takacs, Sarah Parcak, and all of the explorers who every day enlighten, inspire, and challenge us to follow their lead and make the world a better place. I'm grateful to PR gurus Karen Wadsworth and Tracey Mason Daniels of Media Masters and Virginia Anagnos and her team at Goodman Media for their diligent efforts in spreading the word. Finally, thanks to my agent, Rosemary Stimola, who has so deftly steered me through the often treacherous waters of publishing for more than 15 years. She is a beacon of wisdom and kindness. Every writer should be so lucky.